WALLA WALLA SUITE

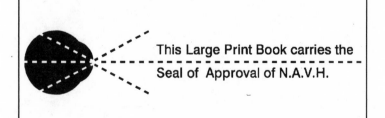

This Large Print Book carries the
Seal of Approval of N.A.V.H.

WALLA WALLA SUITE

(A ROOM WITH NO VIEW)

ANNE ARGULA

THORNDIKE PRESS

An imprint of Thomson Gale, a part of The Thomson Corporation

THOMSON

GALE

Detroit • New York • San Francisco • New Haven, Conn. • Waterville, Maine • London

Thorndike Press® Large Print Mystery.

The text of this Large Print edition is unabridged.

Other aspects of the book may vary from the original edition.

Set in 16 pt. Plantin.

LIBRARY OF CONGRESS CATALOGING-IN-PUBLICATION DATA

Argula, Anne.
  Walla Walla Suite : a room with no view / by Anne Argula.
    p. cm. — (Thorndike Press large print mystery.)
  ISBN-13: 978-1-4104-0420-6 (hardcover : alk. paper)
  ISBN-10: 1-4104-0420-X (hardcover : alk. paper)
    1. Women private investigators — Washington (State) — Walla Walla —
Fiction. 2. Missing persons — Investigation — Fiction. 3. Walla Walla
(Wash.) — Fiction. 4. Large type books. I. Title.
PS3566.O6W35 2008
813'.54—dc22   2007040198

Published in 2008 by arrangement with The Ballantine Publishing Group, a division of Random House, Inc.

Printed in the United States of America on permanent paper
10 9 8 7 6 5 4 3 2 1

For Miami Rose

Tie your shoes and save the drowning.

Henry David Thoreau

■ ■ ■ ■

PART ONE

■ ■ ■ ■

1

Picture this. Instead of sprinkling sand in your eyes the Sandman gives you a shot of liquid fire in the ass. Da frick.

Lying there in the raw, middle of the night, sticking to the sheets, my body was self-basting, my skin tingling like a Christmas goose. Not enough? My head was on a countdown to blow up because some Indians on the street below were beating tribal drums and one of them was torturing a tribal chant. Woi Yesus.

I can't sleep all that well these days, not since losing the company of someone else in the house, that someone else having been my husband, Connors, who finally did what I long expected he would do: leave me for Esther, his pharmacist's assistant. I should care.

When you blow Spokane you can blow it off big, like for LA or Miami or New York, or you can leave small, like for Missoula or

11

Seattle. I left small, but that's mostly because I wanted to leave fast. Funny, because I had pretty much made up my mind that I would never leave the place. Not that I ever liked it that much. In fact, I didn't like it at all, but I had settled in, at least for this lifetime. That was before Connors let his cock run away with his conscience. So I bitch-slapped the city and took it on the arfy-darfy to the upper left-hand corner of the map. Discovering that my husband was bumping uglies with another woman, younger and well oiled, catapulted me to the nearest place large enough to lose myself in, Seattle. Never went back, never going back.

I peeled myself off the bed and moved like a human heat wave to the living room window. On the way I passed by the mirrored wall that still can make me jump, thinking I've seen an intruder. Middle of the night, the light, or lack of it, was in my favor. I couldn't see the veins in my legs, or notice the jiggling parts. Not that I looked that bad, for a woman my age. I sighed. I was taking me as I was becoming. And the hot flashes were killing me.

Both the drum and the chant stopped abruptly, but I was this far so I went to the window anyway. By the time I reached it I was wide awake, and they started up all over again.

I was living alone in a one-bedroom apartment on the eighth floor, Pioneer Square. I'd been there for six months, not all of them good.

The sound of the drum and the chant could have just as easily been coming from inside the room. From inside my head, da frick.

I slid open the window. The night was chilly and damp against my burning face and body, which I was now flashing to Yesler Way. I should care. This time of night, there was nobody there anyway besides those three drunken Indians under the pergola, sprawled all over the bench, their legs splayed this way and that way, gathering themselves for another run at their fading memories. Have at it, boys. Nobody sleeps anymore. It's a national epidemic.

I'd noticed them before, down there, encamping for the night, unwilling to check into one of the missions, or rejected, just as likely, and they were never what you'd call quiet, but this was the first time I heard them singing back to their roots.

The fat one was beating on an overturned city garbage can with a stick. The other fat one had a stick, too, and he beat it against an empty Office Depot box. The skinny one was the singer, who was most frustrated because he couldn't get it right. Empty forties lay scattered at their feet.

"No, that ain't it," said the skinny singer. "How the fuck does it go?"

Their voices carried easily in the still night.

They put their heads together and concentrated, their baseball caps turned backward, their foreheads almost touching. They wore sneakers, and jeans, and though it was cold all they had, the fat ones, were hooded sweatshirts; the singer, a light Windbreaker.

The three beered-up tribals started again, first the ancient drumbeat and then the eerie high-pitched chant that made the hair on the nape of my neck rise up.

Again the singer stumbled. "That ain't it, goddammit." He was hard on himself. Maybe he had moved too far in one direction ever to go back and retrieve something left behind as worthless then, now for some reason damn valuable.

The totem pole loomed behind them on the cobblestones in front of the Pioneer Building, commemorating the settlement that once thrived on that spot, where the ancestors of these three lived off the bounty of the bay and knew how to sing the songs.

The three drunken descendants of those

14

proud and persevering people swatted one another with their caps to remember how the song should be sung. They tried again and this time the singer used his hand to beat the box along with the fat one, to spook out the rhythm that hid from them, to hook back the thing that was lost and floating out there. This time when the singer began to chant, I just knew he had it at last. It filled me with dread and excitement. They've nailed it! They've tapped into their own genetic memories! They remember!

Shit they did. It all fell apart again, sunk under its own psychic weight. The singer looked whipped. I could feel his pain and disappointment all the way up on the eighth floor. He kicked the garbage can and sent it flying. "Fuck! Fuck it all!"

They trudged unsteadily up First Avenue, but one of the drummers staggered back and slung the garbage can over his shoulder. He hurried to catch up with the other two. The singer turned to him and yelled, "Whaddafuck?"

"I'm bringin' the drum."

"That ain't no drum. That's nothin' but a fuckin' garbage can!"

The drum bearer put it down and examined it. The other two kept on plodding up First Avenue. This lagging drummer was

15

slow to leave behind his garbage can, if that's what it was instead of a drum. For a brief moment there, for a measure, it *was* a drum, and he was brave. In the end, though, he left it overturned in the middle of the sidewalk.

A solitary figure crossed First Avenue at Marion to avoid the three drunks.

2

My office, in the Pioneer Building, is just across the street from my apartment. Some of the offices still had lights on. Seattle people are like that: they'll work all night if you let them, maybe just to keep from going outside. I wondered if Vincent Ainge was there at work in his inner office, saving lives, or at least trying to prevent them from being taken away. I'd found him there before in the middle of the night, coming down from my own office.

Vincent saved lives by toiling at words, constructing the one right sentence, much like the tribal singer was trying to find the one perfect rhythm of his chant.

I dialed his office number. I wasn't surprised when he answered, and he was only half surprised that anyone would be calling him at such an hour.

"It's Quinn," I said.

"What's the deal? Can't sleep?"

"Naw. You hear them?"

"Who?"

"The Indians, chanting."

"Indians are chanting?"

"They were, right outside the building. Three drunk ones. They're gone now."

Vincent has an apartment in my building, on the same floor, but his looks out across First Avenue, toward the water. That's how we met, both of us going through the front door at the same time. It was coincidental that we also both had offices in the Pioneer Building and made the commute by elevator and a short walk across the street.

When I got my PI license in King County, after I took early retirement from the Spokane PD and bolted to Seattle, Vincent gave me my first job. It didn't pay spit, but it was easy stuff and I found him interesting, different. I didn't mind working for him. It brought down the odds of some maniac breaking my knees with a bat, and me with no more insurance, and we got along pretty well. We were the same age, humbled to be facing a second half century. I was comfortable with him. It was safe work, I thought. I was wrong.

"Sorry I missed them," he said. "Did they draw a crowd?"

"Only me, standing here naked, burning up."

"And me without a window."

"Who are you working on?"

"Jon."

Where it says *Occupation,* Vincent would write, *Mitigation Investigator.* But I knew he preferred to see himself as a kind of biographer. What separated him from other biographers, forget that his stuff never sees publication, is that all of his subjects, Jon included, are murderers, or suspected murderers.

"Ah, Jon," I said. "What have you got so far?"

"You want to hear it?"

"Can't dance."

He read to me:

Though Jon quit school after the ninth grade, occasioned by substance abuse, truancy, and lack of adult supervision, his art teacher remembers him as having flashes of creativity and an eagerness to learn. He was particularly talented in the area of collages, and even now his cell is decorated with colorful collages assembled from scraps of magazines.

"Aw-w-w," I cooed.

"It's a little thin."

Vincent, Vincent, up in the middle of the

19

night, trying to say something merciful about Jon Kutzmann, age twenty-seven, a pederast whose abuse of young boys had escalated in its dark reach to murder. His previous convictions argued, in Jon's warped mind, for the elimination of witnesses next time around. Jon's explanation for his crimes was, "It just happened." Like shit does. The "whatever" excuse. In Jon's case shit just happened twice. Shit would have just happened a third time but the little boy he tried to lure out of a movie matinee screamed loud and long, exactly as his parents had taught him, and a beefy high school football player brought down Jon three blocks south of the theater and held him for the cops. Two other little boys who hadn't screamed, who'd thought Jon was a friendly adult, had earlier been found in Dumpsters, strangled.

"It's a start, I guess," I said. "Wouldn't turn me around."

As I said, the work was easy, for me, just interviewing old contacts and gathering information favorable to the accused. It was all right until something better came along. My heart wasn't all that into it — not like Vincent, who brought a passion to it that I would never be able to muster. A couple of those guys I'd volunteer to hang personally.

Jon, for an example. Anybody who would kill a child.

"There's an artist on the jury, a middle-aged woman named Janet whose specialty is rhododendrons in watercolors. I'm laying my hopes on her. Jon's talent for collages, pathetic as it is, might be enough to convince the lady artist that he ought to live out his life behind bars without the possibility of parole."

"Devoted to his collages maybe."

"Good news, though. He's found and accepted Jesus."

"Hallelujah," I said drily. "Has Jesus accepted him?"

"Don't knock it, it's a conversion. I plan to make the most of it."

"Good luck."

"It's not enough, is it? Not even for the most evangelical juror."

"For the most evangelical juror it's a salve to his conscience as he sends Jon to the gallows."

"I could sure use something in between."

"Sorry. I couldn't find a soul to say a good word about him. Except for his aunt, and even she —"

"Yeah, and for ten years I got nothing in Jon's life but petty crimes and molestations, a short-lived roofing job, and substance abuse, which is pretty much losing all credibility as a mitigating circumstance."

"Why don't you lie down on the sofa and shut your eyes?"

"Why don't you?"

"I was in bed till I heard the Indians. I'm on my way back there."

"I'll see you in the morning."

I moved away from the window, put the phone back in the cradle, and myself back into bed. I watched the small flames leaping from my toes. I swear I could see them.

Vincent, Vincent, this world was never meant for one as beautiful as you. I could have sung it, and come no closer to the truth than the skinny Indian did.

3

That time of year, the mornings often show up colder than the nights before.

At the side entrance to the Pioneer Building, a picture was taped to the glass door: HAVE YOU SEEN THIS WOMAN?

Below the picture, a name: Eileen Jones. Eighteen years old, missing since Tuesday. Pretty girl, hardly a woman yet. Long blond hair around a roundish face, smiling. She looked vaguely familiar to me. You get used to lost cat, lost dog posters, not that I don't get a little twinge, but lost people always get to me. How can you lose a person? The answer: easy. Of course, sometimes, often, a person loses himself.

I walked from the side entrance down the L-shaped hall to the lobby, where more flyers were posted. There was another one in the old, slow elevator I shared that morning with a man who was, as I was, balancing his breakfast on a Styrofoam cup. In my case a

Belgian waffle atop a double-tall latte, which, by the way, comes to about eight bucks, counting the change dropped into the tip jar, one of which is now everywhere. I'm considering putting one on my desk. We both looked at Eileen's picture while the elevator slowly ascended.

"Nice-looking girl," I said.

"Yeah."

"She work in the building, you know?"

"Yes."

"I figured. Who for?"

"Arnie Stimick, on the sixth floor."

"What happened, you know?" I asked the stranger.

"Just that she left the office after work Tuesday and nobody's seen her since. Her car's missing, too."

"My name's Quinn. Fifth floor. Private investigator."

I switched my breakfast to my left hand and extended my right. He did the same thing.

"Ronnie Culson. Sixth floor. I'm an architect. Maybe you can find her."

"How's that?"

"You're a detective, right?"

"Oh, yeah."

The elevator stopped at the fourth floor and I got off. The man said, "This is only the fourth floor."

"Yeah, I know that."

The door closed and the man kept rising.

The building was more than a hundred years old, one of the oldest buildings in the city, in the oldest neighborhood of the city. Rents were cheap because of a downtown boom during which they built too many office buildings.

We were an odd bunch there. Entrepreneurs, some fly-by-night, others ill adapted to the business world; rumpled lawyers unable or unwilling to join a firm; off-brand insurance peddlers; young computer geeks, late of Silicon Valley; nervous accountants; visionary graphic designers; at least one slightly confused architect, I'd just found out, and a couple of people I suppose I could call friends. Vincent, of course, and Bernard, who used to be a gangbanger, an LA Crip with the street name Romeo, but now a respectable ticket scalper and the only black dude in the building. I think. At least I haven't seen any others. He's outgoing, Bernard, and likable, slick and wiry, the kind of kid bigger thugs like to use to break into a store via the air vent. He struck up a conversation with me and in no time told me that things were too hot for him in Los Angeles so he boogied on up north and fell in love with the city. What he meant, I think, was that Seattlites were at heart naïve and it was easy for him to make a semi-legitimate living. Anyway, after that, whenever he saw me he would treat me like a friend and so I treated him the same way. He knows I'm an ex-cop and he thinks that's hysterical for some reason, like we've both turned over a new leaf.

I knew nothing was waiting for me in my office, so I went to Vincent's to finish my breakfast. His door was ajar. I stood for a moment in the doorway. He was all bent over his desk, lost in his work. He had a full beard and unruly hair. A big guy, six feet, maybe two hundred pounds, but small in his own mind. He looked like he worked out, but I never saw him work out and he never talked about a gym. He was wearing a denim shirt and his reading glasses. His office was small and windowless. The wall behind him was brick. The only source of natural light came from the skylight at my back, where, when there was any, light came flooding down through the open atrium that extended from roof to first floor, including through his door if he left it open.

That skylight is supposed to be the first one in America, only one of the many firsts claimed by Seattle, like the first electric

26

guitar, the invention of waterskiing, Twinkies, Gore-Tex, Starbucks, and, of course, the first suicide hotline, still the busiest.

I happen to have a window in my own office, and outside on the ledge I've installed Stanley the Snake, a long plastic reptile whose job is to scare away the pigeons, and Stanley's doing well, thank you. Vincent's rent was cheaper, but that wasn't why he didn't have any windows. I think he had a need for enclosure.

Vincent was an Evergreen alum, the famous touchy-feely college in the woods, where he discovered he was a Wordsworthian and thus lost to the world of business. He knew that he could never work for a profit-making organization, but he did not know what trade he might ply. He was willing, determined even, to follow his bliss, but he couldn't pin down what that was. The University of Washington, U-Dub, followed, on a scholarship, and with a master's in social work in hand he hired on with King County as a caseworker, assistance to the aged, then on to juvenile hall, where on his own he started to construct specific programs for specific offenders, a practice that seemed to work but could get no official support. He left the bureaucracy and set up a private practice. In the beginning he was forced to sell his services to the well-off, setting up for their children detailed programs for education, community service, and career planning, including disciplined schedules of self-examination, all for a hefty fee, beginning as soon as possible after the initial arrest, so that Vincent's advance planning could be used to preclude jail time, if not a trial itself. For his own survival, he had to work for the wealthy, who were only too happy to pay his rates if it kept Junior out of the big house, but as soon as Vincent was able he took on more and more pro bono work. It was a natural step, when the idea occurred to him, to take on mitigation factors in capital cases. Once started, he couldn't stop.

His hand blindly searched the desk for his Starbucks cup of latte. Finally he had to look up to find it and that's when he saw me.

"Quinn? How long have you been standing there?"

"Orange. Pencil. Baseball," I said.

"Got it."

It was a game we played. To see if we were any closer to losing our minds. He took the game more seriously than I did, for good reason. His father had Alzheimer's disease.

"Why don't you treat yourself to a window?" I asked him.

"Don't need one."

"I know you don't need one, but wouldn't it be pleasant to have one?"

"Not that pleasant."

"Unless you're afraid of jumping out of it."

"Always a possibility."

I sat in his cushioned wicker chair, a thing of no beauty and only passing comfort.

"I would have brought you a latte."

"I already have one."

"That's why I didn't."

"Sit down."

"I am sitting down."

"Oh."

"Still working on Jon?"

"He is a challenge."

"You see the posters on the missing girl?"

"I have. Do you know her?"

"No. You?"

"I ran into her once."

"How?"

"I saw her downstairs. Maybe a month ago. It was cold out and drizzling."

"It is now."

"I was going to the FedEx kiosk, picking up some forms and envelopes. She was leaning against the wall, smoking a cigarette."

"You're not supposed to smoke in the

building."

"I know. So did she. She smiled at me. I've always been refreshed by a natural smile, a smile that doesn't want anything, that isn't calculated."

"I didn't know that about you."

"Teenage girls, lots of them, have smiles like that. It's delightful."

"Whoa. Teenage girls? Is this a subject you know something about?"

"I don't know anything about them. About women in general."

"So she smiled at you. Then what?"

"She said, 'They don't let you smoke in my office.' "

"Like I said."

" 'It's like that everywhere now,' I said to her. I might have smiled myself."

"You're not famous for that."

"I smile."

I heard it as *ice mile.* Probably closer to the truth. A long cold way to go.

"Maybe you're just not around when I do," he said.

"Maybe you only do it at teenage girls, for all I know."

"She said, and I'm sure of this, she said, 'My boss is pretty anal about smoking.' She giggled when she said that. It was pretty funny. It was a small burst of joyful conspiracy, peculiar to teenage girls."

"There you go again. Are you gaga over young pussy like all the rest of 'em?"

"Quinn, please."

"Well, you got to wonder."

"I have not had pussy since pussy's had me."

Now even I had to laugh, even though I couldn't do it like she did. I should care.

"Young for me, I recently calculated, is thirty-eight," he said. "And I would be thrilled."

"So what else did she say, your smiley teenager?"

"She said, 'Somebody told me that foreigners, tourists from Europe, see all these girls, office and shopgirls, hanging outside, smoking cigarettes, and they think they must all be prostitutes.' "

"Tourists from Europe, in Seattle?"

"Sure. They come. They hear stuff, they want to see for themselves. Jimi Hendrix. Bruce Lee. They want to visit the first Starbucks and have their pictures taken in front of it. And I don't know about you but I take some personal pride in knowing that the richest man in the world, who could live wherever he pleases, chooses to live right here."

"Yeah, well, he was born and raised here,

like you."

"Then why aren't you where you were born and raised? Where was it, Shenandoah, Pennsylvania?"

"It's a long story. I dream of it, though. The secret beauty of hard coal."

"No, you're one of us now. I can tell. You like the gray, the wet, even the mold."

"It's growing on me. Just on my north side. So that was the whole encounter?"

"With the missing girl?"

"Eileen Jones is her name."

"No, I'm only halfway through it."

"Well, then you knew her pretty goddamn good. You were, like, intimate."

"Quit playing detective."

"I *am* a detective. I thought you knew that."

"I don't know where she is."

"But you knew her pretty good. I'm a detective, you're now a person of interest."

"I saw her once. She stayed in my memory. I knew her well enough not to rat her out. That's what she said, 'You won't rat me out, will you?' I assured her I was no squealer. 'It's just too miserable to be outside,' she said. I told her I smoked an occasional cigar myself."

"Why did you tell her that?"

"I wanted her to think we had something

in common."

"What did she say?"

"Yuk."

"She said 'yuk'?"

"Yuk."

"So you had nothing in common."

"I knew I had lost her. Any fantasy I might have had. It happens that way. You meet a pretty young girl and say casually that a big Friday night for you is sitting down in your stocking feet with a pig's foot and a long-neck Bud. Any chance you ever had goes out the window."

"You think there was any chance to begin with?"

"No, of course not."

"It doesn't stop you dogs, though. You keep on making fools of yourselves."

"It's a curse."

"On who?"

He scratched his fingers through his beard.

"I thought she must be somebody's secretary. I've never had a secretary. Wouldn't know what to do with one. I would probably become emotionally involved with one."

"Definitely."

"I might even become obsessed with one, if I had a secretary, if she was too pretty or winning. And where would I put her? Besides, I'm too accustomed to doing things for myself, even the most trivial things."

"Those are the things you enjoy the most."

"That's true. When I file, for instance. I love it. It frees up my mind wonderfully."

"Yeah, like for what?"

He thought about it for a moment, scratched his beard again.

"So I can remember where I left my cell phone?"

"Then where is it?"

"What?"

"Your cell phone."

He patted his pockets.

"I don't know. In my car, probably."

He gave me a sheepish grin.

"So that was it? With the girl?"

"Pretty much. We probably talked for another few minutes. She tossed her cigarette and I got my FedEx stuff."

"Did you ride up in the elevator together?"

"No . . . I may have ducked out for a latte."

"What if she's dead now, that girl you talked to?"

"Why would she be dead? It's only been two days. One day, two nights."

"If you're a girl and you're missing . . . for two nights, you could be dead. That's city life in America. Country life, too, for that matter."

"She could be on an adventure. She's young, with impulses, passions."

"What kind of impulses and passions?"

"She might have self-doubts . . . or over-confidence, fear or bravado, all kinds of mixed emotions boiling over."

"You know a little too much about teeny-boppers, in my opinion."

"You make her sound like she was twelve. She was a grown woman. She might have decided to jump on a plane and fly to . . . Tahiti."

"Tahiti?"

"That's where I would go."

"You're not the one's missing."

"I'm saying she might have had an impulse to go somewhere."

"That's your professional deduction?"

"Given what we know. What's yours?"

"She left here after work Tuesday, rainy night, walked across James Street to the parking lot, and nobody's seen her or her car since. That's all I know. Only . . . you notice her hair? I don't know why, but they always go for the girls with long hair."

"Who?"

"Your friends, the sexual predators."

"Quinn, it's too early in the morning for you to be busting my balls."

"You think I'm busting your balls? Now?

You don't know me very well."

"Sexual predators are not my friends. And you're wrong about them always going for girls with long hair."

"You'll notice I keep mine short."

"I thought you said you couldn't grow it anymore. The menopause penalty."

"I told you that?"

"I've never told anyone else."

"Well, don't."

"Quinn, Quinn, Quinn . . ."

"Quinn yourself."

"This girl, Eileen, she could have had an accident. The car could have gone off the highway, rolled over out of sight . . ."

"Where's she live?"

"Magnolia, with a roommate. A girl she went to high school with."

"You knew that?"

"She mentioned it."

"So between here and Magnolia she's gonna roll off the road and out of sight? Never happen."

I flipped my empty coffee cup into his trash basket.

Vincent stared at a spot somewhere over my head.

"Eighteen," he said finally.

"What?"

"She's only eighteen. All eighteen-year-old girls are beautiful, don't you think?"

"Jesus . . . men."

"They are, each one special, in her own way. They're adorable, in the true sense of that word. I believe she's going to show up. Eighteen-year-old girls can be very dramatic."

"Yeah, like the predators who stalk them, your poor misunderstood."

"We're all misunderstood, why should they be any different?"

"Like your friend Jon?" I said, needling him a little. I knew he hated Jon.

"Remember his aunt?"

I had found the aunt for him. When Jon was a child his mother dropped him with her for a year while she went through detox and a serious program, both of which were less than successful.

"Let's call her up."

"Go ahead."

He put it on speakerphone and dialed the number.

"Mrs. Chelmsford? This is Vincent Ainge, I spoke to you before. I'm working on your nephew's case."

"Will it never end?" she said. A heavy weariness thickened her voice.

"We're getting to the end of the trial, another couple of days at most. It doesn't look good, Mrs. Chelmsford, for Jon. It looks pretty bad, in fact. They're going to find him guilty, ma'am, and then they will start up the penalty phase of the trial. That's when it becomes a matter of life and death."

"Nothin' I can do about it."

"Well, that's not necessarily true, ma'am."

"I told you all I know, last time."

"Yes, ma'am, and it's the sort of thing we would like the jury to hear. But it would be so much better if they could hear it from you. We want you to tell them the condition Jon was in when he was left with you, the abuse, you know, the bruises and everything, and the rags he was wearing, how he couldn't talk. We'd like the jurors to hear just what kind of kid Jon was while he lived with you. He was an okay kid then. And they should know what you know about his mother and his father."

"His mother was a crack whore and his father was a drug pusher. I told you all that."

"Yes, ma'am, but it's really important you tell that to the jury."

"You tell 'em. I'm a tired old lady. I don't want no more to do with this. I'm sick over this."

I drew the edge of my hand across my throat. Enough. No point pushing her.

Vincent nodded and ended the conversation.

"You think she'd be any good anyway?" I asked.

"Anyone who loved him would be good."

"I'm not sure she ever did."

"I think she did. She raised him for a year. I think she loved him then. She's possibly the only one who ever did."

"I'm off. Let's have the words," I said, meaning the three words I'd given him when I showed up in his doorway.

He said *orange* straightaway, but he had to take a moment to remember before he said, *"Pencil . . ."*

"Two for two. One more to go."

He couldn't remember the third word. He looked distressed. I gave him a break. "It's a sport," I said.

"Baseball!" he cried out.

"Congratulations. You don't have Alzheimer's."

"Baseball. A game I could never understand."

"What's to understand?"

"To me, it's a dull exercise full of meaningless posturings, sparked by exciting moments few and far between."

"Sounds good."

"Mariners' fans have to approach the

39

game with a Zen-like detachment, unconcerned about winning because they seldom do. It is a game that requires . . . of course! Concentration!"

The joke was on him, seemed like. I didn't get it.

4

It rained for most of the morning and then the gray went soft, like a fireside-and-coffee gray, a falling-asleep kind of gray. The streets were washed clean of derelict spit. I took advantage of the break in the weather and walked up to the Public Market for lunch. You know the tiny burrito window that fronts on First Avenue? That's where I stood in line for a veggie burrito. I'm partial to them. Growing up in Shenandoah, Pennsylvania, I never met a Mexican, had no idea what a burrito was until I hit LA. Back in the hard-coal regions, we ate halupkies, halushkis, babkas, bleenies, food like that. Now, I hear, there is a Latin American "community" there and a couple of good Mexican restaurants. It's the new wave of immigrants, and I'm hoping they will bring the place back to life, whatever flavor it turns out to be. Shenandoah's always been a town with a heavy accent anyway. The accent might as well be Mexican.

I went around the corner and ate my burrito leaning against the statue of the pig. I watched the fishmongers toss great king salmon through the air to be weighed and wrapped and sent home in dry ice with visiting businessmen.

I wasn't having such a bad time, to tell you the truth, despite being on fire half the time. Suddenly single is no glide, especially the way it landed on me. "I'm in love with Esther." Go fester. I never gave myself a chance to get off the floor before taking early retirement and bugging out of Spokane, but I was doing all right. I missed my old partner, Odd Gunderson, though we stay in touch by phone. I missed the comfort of my own house, in which now lives a family moved in from Coeur d'Alene. But all in all things weren't so bad. I had my retirement and a monthly from Connors and I was making a little on my own, hoping to make more once I was established. I'd made myself a nest in Pioneer Square, I'd opened up shop as a PI, and Vincent was growing on me. I had a friend. I didn't share his passion for saving the lives of the worthless, because I know that one life follows another and everybody gets to sort it out for himself, no matter how long it takes or how many times he turns out to be a scumbag. I wondered from time to time if Vincent and I had known each other in a previous life, like Odd and I had. Could be.

After my lunch I walked back through the southernmost end of the market and dropped downstairs to Shorey's Books to browse a bit. I made a find, a copy of a 1933 handbook bound in suede. *Scientific Murder Investigation,* by Luke S. May. I read around in it. One section was titled "Motive."

MOTIVES FOR THE CRIME OF MURDER:

1. As part of another crime
2. To conceal another crime
3. Financial gain
4. Hate
5. Superstition
6. Jealousy
7. Envy
8. Accidental
9. Quarrel
10. Love
11. Revenge
12. Escape
13. Lust
14. Secure safety of Murderer
15. Fear of exposure
16. Undue correction for Misconduct

17. Necessity (self-preservation)
18. Unhappy matrimonial relations
19. Insane desire to kill
20. Witchcraft
21. Religious sacrifice
22. Preventing victim from doing some particular thing
23. Recovery of property taken by victim
24. Cannibalism
25. Fancied wrong
26. Political
27. Protection of others
28. Malpractice
29. Blackmail

Woi Yesus! So many reasons for murdering another human being. And it was a very old book. There might be more now, motives that Detective May could not have anticipated all those years ago, while making his list. A desire to be on TV, for one example. A need to be noticed.

With the book paid for and in my pocket, I went out to the street. It was drizzling again, but I wasn't far from my office, and I don't mind walking in the rain. It cools the flames shooting out of my ears.

5

I sat in my office reading the old book on murder investigation. You never know, I might have to investigate a murder someday. Yeah, right. There was that one, but Odd and I fell into that, just two dumb cops, and we had help from an inside source, so to speak. I wrote a book about it, which most people didn't believe anyway. Why should they?

A knock on the door. Me, in my most professional voice, hoping for a walk-in: "C'mon in, it's open."

It was Bernard, wearing a woolly cap pulled down over his forehead.

"Oh, it's you."

"That's cold, man. I thought you liked me."

"Sorry. I was hoping you were a paying customer."

"I'm hoping the same thing. I got two tickets, dirt cheap, for Death Cab for Cutie."

"Say what?"

"You don't know them?"

"If it ain't the Rolling Stones, I don't know them."

"Up-and-coming group. You'll love 'em."

"I will not."

"I'm telling you as a friend, you ought to get out more. I'd take you myself, but I'm working."

"Don't do me any favors. I hate concerts."

"Wha . . . ? Everybody loves concerts."

"I hate the way people stand up in front of me, waving their arms, like it's all about them. Pay me, I might go to another concert."

"You know anybody who, like, likes to go out?"

Bernard was always on the hustle, walked with a phone in his ear.

"Bernard . . . you see the posters, of the missing girl?"

"Yeah, man . . . they're all over."

"Did you know her?"

"What do you mean?"

"It's not a trick question."

"I was in my office, man, workin'. I can show you phone records."

"Da frick, Bernard. Don't be so paranoid. Nobody's accusing you of anything."

"Not yet."

"You're so paranoid."

"That the word?"

"C'mon, get off it."

"I knew her, Quinn. Okay? She was into me."

"Was? And how far?"

"If she's gone, man, it's *was*. I was interested, I ain't gonna say I wasn't. But she was way too young, and kinda, you know, different."

"How different?"

"Silly, like."

"Wild?"

"No, that I could get down with. Girlish. Stupid, like. Fine-lookin' thing, but . . . let's put it this way. I didn't need the distraction. She was not someone I wanted to get all, you know, with, okay?"

"You date her?"

He laughed. "Comin' from you, I don't even know what that means?"

"It's not complicated. Dinner together, a movie . . . a concert maybe."

"You're like a mother, aren't you?"

"Definitely. I got a son in the navy."

"No, Quinn, never did any of that, or anything else, either. Only every time we passed in the hall or rode the elevator together, she came on to me."

"Okay, I'm beginning to get the picture.

She said hello a couple of times and you thought she wanted to jump your bones."

He laughed again. "Can I call you Mama?"

"Can I break your fuckin' jaw?"

I was entertaining the hell out of him, but he was the only one laughing.

"It's like the old joke," I said. "You: I almost got laid last night. Me: Oh, yeah? What happened? You: She said no."

"Nice talkin' to you, Quinn. When you gonna buy a ticket for something?"

I stopped him before he could leave.

"Bernard, you know where the girl worked?"

"Yeah, sixth floor. For Arnie Stimick."

"What's his deal?"

"He's a promoter. Mostly, he runs testimonial dinners."

"Who for?"

"Anybody . . . union bosses, politicians, top cops and firemen, like that. Like when they retire and stuff."

"There's a living in that?"

"Fuck, no. But there's a nice taste in printing the programs for the testimonials. You want to know why?"

"I'm in this far."

"Because his girls sell the advertising for in the programs, along with the tickets to the dinner, usually to people who can't say no, because they do business with the honoree. You follow me?"

"Yeah, I get it."

"And he gets to know the right people, you know, which always means money down the line."

"Keep in touch, Bernard."

"Sometimes, man, you still sound like a cop."

He shut the door behind him. I felt oddly flattered.

6

I was walking the corridors, trying to squelch another hot flash. I'd already gone to the ladies' and splashed my face and the back of my neck with cold water. It's hard to sit still when your ass is on fire, not that my feet were that much cooler. Da frick.

Hardly aware I was doing it, I buzzed for the elevator, then — too impatient to wait — I walked up the stairs to the sixth floor and found my way to what I thought had to be Arnie Stimick's door: PROMOTION IN MOTION. Cute.

I opened the door. In the outer office three girls in cubicles the size of broom closets were on phones, wearing headsets and twirling pencils between their fingers. They looked up at me when I entered. I stood at the door. One cubicle was vacant.

To a girl they looked more or less like Eileen. Eighteen, twenty, maybe twenty-one, the old-timer. Varying shades of blond hair worn long. Meat on their bones, faces slightly rounded.

"Can I help you?" one of them said to me, her phone conversation just over.

Good question. I didn't even know why I was there, except looking for a cool spot.

"Was that one Eileen's?" I asked, nodding to the empty cubicle.

"Yes," she said, and some of the color drained from her face.

"You all right?"

"Have they found her?" She was frightened, poor thing. The other girls stopped talking and looked at me.

I guess I do look like a cop. I told them I wasn't one. Why bother telling them I used to be, and old habits are hard to break? I told them I worked in the building and was concerned. Most of us were. The two went back to their phone pitches. The other held off and talked to me.

"We're all so scared. We keep hoping . . ."

"It could turn out all right."

"Arnie walks us to our cars or our buses now. He feels so guilty 'cause he didn't walk Eileen to her car that night."

"What happened could have happened after she got into her car, after she drove away, or maybe she stopped somewhere. If anything happened at all. Maybe nothing

51

happened."

"I guess," she said, not put at ease, but I don't do that.

It's that two-level open parking lot that rises to a point, like the prow of a ship, splitting Yesler Way and James Street. It's ominous, somehow. You can imagine bad things happening there, even though the top tier is wide open, in view of hundreds of office windows. The lower tier has dark corners smelling of urine, but even there most of the cars are visible to at least a saloon, a Korean deli, and the pergola, not to mention anyone walking up Yesler or down James. That observed, I still wouldn't want to park there. That's where it must've happened, if anything had happened to Eileen.

"I understand she lives in the Magnolia area?"

"Yes, she has a roommate, a girl she went to high school with."

"Any boyfriends?"

"She has a kind of a boyfriend. His name is Guy. God, I hope she's all right."

"Have the police talked to them, the roommate and the boyfriend?"

"Don't know. Must have. They talked to us. Arnie knows most of them and he's pressing them hard to find her."

The door to the inner office opened and

the space filled up with the imposing figure of Arnie Stimick. Boonda brute in an expensive Filson shirt, six-five and every bit of 275 pounds. Bald on the top, thin black hair on the sides, turning gray. He was wearing glasses and one of those beards that look like the dude just forgot to shave for a few days, but it's there really to hide the chins. He was nothing if not forthright.

"Who the hell are you?" he said.

7

So I sat across the desk from Arnie Stimick and gave him my story, the short version. He gave me his, even shorter. From back east, like me. A degree from Syracuse, thanks to a basketball scholarship. It was kind of hard to picture him dribbling a ball or going up for a rebound, let alone driving and scoring, but the years will lard you up if you let them. Maybe he was making more out of himself than he ever was. I should care. Men do that. I can't tell you how many ex–Navy SEALs I dated in LA. Most of them I could have dropped with one punch, and a couple of them I did. After college, Stimick told me, he went to Manhattan and got into show business, small musical revues, retro vaudeville stuff. I didn't ask for details. Dancing girls may have been involved. I asked him about the girls in the outer office, where there used to be Eileen Jones, whereabouts now unknown.

"They call themselves Arnie's Angels." He smiled. "We're like family. They're good kids. I'll never forgive myself if . . ."

I could have finished his sentence but I didn't.

"The police are on it?"

"Yeah, they're doing the best they can, for me. I do a lot of shows for them. But I'm worried they think she just took off and in a few days she'll show up again."

"It's possible. It's happened before. It's what usually happens, ain't it?"

"No, not with Eileen. She was a sensible girl, had a good head on her shoulders."

I remember Bernard called her silly, but I was more inclined to accept Stimick's take on the girl. I was kind of looking for a way to leave, but Stimick acted like he needed someone to talk to, or at. He shut the lid on his laptop, then opened it again.

"You want a cup of coffee?" he asked.

"No, thanks. Maybe she had a fight with her boyfriend, something like that."

"Boyfriend?"

"Guy something."

"Oh, him. That was nothing. She didn't care about him."

"Really?"

"He came here once, lunchtime, and she was embarrassed he showed up. Ashamed to introduce him to us. Grungy kid in torn jeans. You wanna hear his plan for the future?"

"He had one?"

"Trying to get the band back together, that was his prospects. Eileen was way ahead of that. He was harmless, but useless, too."

"Well, it's only been two days," I said, showing an optimism I had only on loan. I put my hands on the arms of my chair and made like to rise.

"Listen, Quinn . . . is that your first name or your last name?"

"It's both."

"I hear you."

What he heard, I guess, was that we were both professionals.

"I'm a professional, Quinn, and I can see you are, too. I got a good feel for people. Meeting you like this is fortuitous. I don't know why I didn't think of it before."

"Think of what? Before what?"

"A private detective. I guess I thought the police . . . but, you know the police, sometimes they have too much to do. Do you have too much to do?"

If he only knew. All I'd been doing is searching out people who might have a kind word to say about some yonko facing trial for murder.

"I didn't come to solicit you for business, Mr. Stimick." Maybe I did. I couldn't tell him I was just walking off a killer hot flash. "I was just concerned, and curious."

"Call me Arnie, please. And I know you didn't come up here looking for business. I can appreciate the whole building is upset about this, but, hey, here you are, you're a detective and we've got a missing girl. How about it? Can you find her for us?"

"I can try. But should you be the one doing the hiring . . . and the paying? What about her family?"

"It's just her mom, and she's recently divorced. Her dad lives in Hawaii now. Look, I want to, I can afford it. You bring her back safe and sound, it'll be the best money I ever spent. This office won't ever be the same without her."

It would be my first real job in Seattle, my first as a PI, not counting all the stuff I'd been doing for Vincent, which I kind of wanted to get out of anyway. I told Arnie we were in business and I would bring up my standard one-page contract. So instead of getting up I settled in again. Up to now it was a little more than small talk but it was still just surface skipping.

"You're going to want to talk to the cops,"

he said, "see what they have, coordinate. I'll make the call for you. See a Sergeant Beckman, he'll give you anything you want."

"Thanks. I'll do that."

"Soon as you leave, I'll call him."

"How long has Eileen been working here?" I asked him.

"Right after graduation from high school, around eight months. She already got a raise."

"So what's she making now?"

"A little north of fifteen an hour."

"That's pretty good for a kid just out of high school."

"Worth every penny of it. I pay all my girls well. It just makes sense."

"She had her own car?"

"A silver Camry, about eight years old. I can get you the plate number."

The Camry has long been the car of choice for thieves.

I asked him for her cell phone number, some other details he had knowledge of, some he didn't, standard stuff. Before I left I spent some more time with the girls, just to get their impressions. All of which would pretty much get me nowhere, but . . . it was a start. I was on the job.

8

The farther out you go, the cheaper the rents, but no kid wants to go much farther out than Magnolia. Farther than that, you might as well be in Everett. I followed the course I imagined Eileen would have taken to go home after work. It all looked good to me. I got lost a couple of times before I found her apartment. When I finally got to the door, I heard some headbanger music from within. I put a hard rap on the door. The music went down and I heard some whispering. A girl's voice came through the door.

"Who is it?" She sounded frightened.

"My name is Quinn. I'm working on Eileen's disappearance."

"Are you a cop?" Now she sounded more frightened. "Because the cops were already here and everything."

"Private investigator, hired by her boss."

She opened the door a crack. I saw something move behind her.

"Arnie hired you?"

"That's right. You know Arnie?"

"Not personally. Can I see some ID?"

Smart girl. I showed her some.

"Okay. I'm a little weirded, you know."

"I understand."

"What do you want to know?"

"Can I come in . . . or is this a bad time?"

She thought about it, and while she thought about it, bad time or not, I was in. The reason for her hesitancy was sitting on the davy, a young man in a wifebeater shirt with the tattoo on his bicep of, near as I could tell, a vortex with the words: BLESSED OBLIVION. Maybe it was the name of his band. Maybe a personal philosophy. It was too cold for what he was wearing. I looked around for a real shirt. Blessed Oblivion was flipping through some CDs. His hair was longer than hers, and a little farther distant from a shampoo.

"This is Mrs. Quinn," she told him. "She's a private eye."

She couldn't contain herself. A giggle spurted out and it infected him.

"Just Quinn," I said, and gave them a minute to get over it. Whatever hand waving they had done when I showed up and knocked on the door didn't dispel the aroma of a hay field hanging in the air. "You guys high?"

"I'm sorry, what do you mean?" she said, and clamped down on her own lip to keep from peeing her pants. Wifebeater put his nose close to a CD of sudden interest.

"Relax. I couldn't bust you if I wanted to, which I don't."

"You want a hit?"

"Maybe later."

I sat down. No one was going to introduce the boy, so I did it myself.

"How're you doing, Guy?"

His head jerked back. "How do you know my name?"

"Fifty–fifty chance. I figured you were either her boyfriend" — nodding to the roommate — "or Eileen's."

"I don't have any boyfriend," she said quickly.

I should care. I found out her name was Darla and she worked at Old Navy downtown. Eileen made twice the money she did and could have afforded an apartment of her own, but she preferred to room with Darla. Guy was a part-time barista at the Starbucks on Second Avenue in the Belltown neighborhood, that one across the street from the new big upscale condo development. I inquired once again after his emotional state.

"It's a little scary," he said.

"Totally," said Darla, raising the ante.

"Be's having a hand to hold helps, ain't?"

"Huh?"

I never know whether it's my coal-cracker patois, which kicks in without any warning, or other people's tilt toward the oblique. I'm not all that foggy, me.

"At times like this mutual friends comfort each other," I signified.

"Oh, yeah," said Guy, and she totaled him once again.

"But I don't get why you're scared."

"Not scared exactly. Freaked. A little. I mean, where the hell is she? She didn't just vanish."

"People do. It's not against the law."

"You have to have a reason, though. Eileen didn't have a reason."

"None that we know about. Yet."

I asked more questions, about Eileen. Her habits, her personality, her friends and foes. Truth is, I didn't really know what I was doing. Just feeling my way.

"Everybody liked Eileen, is what I'm hearing," I said.

Darla said, what else, "Totally. She doesn't even have bad thoughts."

"How do you know that?"

"She would have told me."

"She told you everything?"

"Well . . . I guess I don't know, but she never said a bad word about anyone . . . or anything."

"She doesn't let negative things stay in her mind," said her boyfriend. "She tries to find the best in everything."

"Including you?"

"Yeah, it's, like, overwhelming sometimes."

"How do you mean?"

"She won't let me be an asshole, even if I try. I can do or say something stupid or mean and she might get mad for a minute and then shake it off, and think about the good things, and remind me about the good things, the good things about *me*. Not just me, she does that with everybody. It's not what you expect. It throws you sometimes."

"I'd like someone like that around," I said.

"Yeah."

"Who wouldn't?"

"Right."

"And she's very pretty. I've seen pictures."

"She's beautiful."

"How serious was it between you two?"

"Pretty serious. We're both young, so . . . but I'm serious."

Darla had a ragged fingernail.

"Did she have her own room in here?"

"Yes," she said, "it's a two-bedroom apartment."

That's when she told me about how Eileen could afford to have her own place but didn't want to live alone.

"What about moving in with you?" I asked Guy.

Darla laughed and said, "He practically lives here anyway."

"I live with two guys over in Georgetown," he said.

"Can I see it?"

"See what?"

"Her bedroom."

Darla opened the door and stood in the doorway watching me. Guy stayed on the davy, maybe too stoned to get up, or seeing no good reason to bother.

It was a small room, but with a big bed, a king size, with pillows piled against the headboard. The bed took up most of the room. Apart from that, you see one young girl's room, you've seen them all. She had a laptop on a thing that did double, maybe triple duty as a vanity, desk, and sewing table. There was something under a crocheted cover. I lifted the cover, turned to Darla.

"A sewing machine?"

"Yeah, Eileen sews. I don't mean just fixing rips and putting on buttons. She *makes* stuff. She has dreams of designing a line of clothes."

"I hope her dreams come true."

"Oh, I didn't mean . . ."

"That's all right. You can't help thinking about the worst."

"God, I have nightmares."

I opened the lid on her laptop and hit the space bar. The machine was shut down.

"Did she always shut down her computer at the end of the day?"

"I don't know."

"I leave mine on all the time."

"So do I."

"She ever tell you the password to her computer?" I asked.

"No."

"So she didn't tell you everything."

"Not that."

"When you're straight you should sit down and think of the possibilities. For a password. Try some out on her computer."

"Why?"

"It might help to see her last e-mails, received and sent."

"Oh. Okay."

I opened the closet, two sliding mirrored doors. A rack of shoes, clothes on hangers, tightly packed, a shelf of boxes up above.

"Eileen wouldn't like a stranger going through her closet."

Was there a secret in there, something I wasn't supposed to see? Or was she saying only what's generally true. Hell, I wouldn't want a stranger going through my closet . . . unless I was missing and somebody wanted to find me.

"Should I not go through it?"

"I'm just saying."

"Could you tell by looking if something is missing? From her closet."

"I don't know. I haven't looked."

"Maybe when you're straight you can look."

"I am straight, just about."

I gave her my card. "Call me if you think of anything. Did she ever talk about going to a place, you know, a dream place, the place she hoped to go to someday."

"New York, I guess. Guy?"

"New York, for sure." Guy got off the davy and came to the end of the hallway.

"You think she went to New York?" asked Darla. "Drove her car to New York?"

"It doesn't look like it. But if she did take off by herself, for any reason, then New York might be a place she would take off to."

"But you don't think she did."

"Naw. What was she wearing that day?"

"Her raincoat, is all I remember. It was raining. Knee length, navy blue . . . and black boots. Guy?"

"A skirt."

"You were here? That morning?"

"Yeah. I spent the night."

"He does that sometimes. It's all right with me," said Darla.

"What color skirt?"

"I don't know. I'm color blind. So it was probably greenish."

"You saw her dress?"

"A skirt, I said."

"No, I mean you saw her put on her clothes."

"Oh, yeah. I stay in bed a little longer."

"I leave later, too," said Darla. "So when I saw her go, all I remember is the raincoat and the boots."

"What else? What kind of top?"

"A sweater. Long sleeves. Looked real nice on her. Black, I think. Or dark navy or like that."

I stood in her room a little longer, hoping something would leap out at me and say, Here, stupid, here's what will find her.

"I'll go now," I said at last. "You'll call me if you think of anything, ain't?"

"Totally."

"Can I use your bathroom first?"

"Sure." She opened the door. It was right next to the bedroom.

Once inside, I heard the music come up again. They were back in the living room and didn't want me to hear them. Which was fine by me because I didn't want them to hear me, either. I rifled the sink cabinet. Nothing unusual going on there, except in the back of one drawer I found a package of condoms, the large economy box. It had been broken open and it looked like the items were moving out of stock.

I lifted the lid of the toilet on the off chance I might find a freshly spent one. Didn't happen, but there floating in the water was a half-gone cigarette, filter tip. I hadn't seen any ashtrays in the house, nor signs that the other two smoked . . . tobacco. I looked at it for a moment, bent closer and tried to detect lipstick on the filter. I thought about fishing it out, but then thought better of it. What the hell would I do with it?

In the medicine cabinet I saw a wheel of birth control pills, in Darla's name. These girls were taking no chances, at least one of them wasn't. For all I knew, the other had already taken one chance too many.

It's possible Eileen wasn't on the pill, but that possibility seemed slim. If she was, where were they? I couldn't go back to the bedroom and look through those drawers. Besides, everybody keeps them in the bathroom. I did, unless I was anticipating an overnighter, at which time I carried them in my purse. So if they were in Eileen's purse, she may have had plans that didn't include the future rock star stoned on the davy. Or else she had no plans but kept her pills with her routinely, should something unexpected pop up. I didn't much believe that, though. Purses are always falling open, or things are thrown out in a hurry to find something else, giving rise to moments of embarrassment when your wheel of pills rolls out on the table. A diaphragm is a whole other matter. That puppy has to ride along with you, discovery be damned, but I wondered if young girls today even bothered with diaphragms, romance killers if ever there were any. Only shows how much I had lost touch with being a woman with a fire where a fire ought to be.

I came out and thanked them for seeing me and answering my questions. I wished them good night and went for the door, stopping and making a show of looking through my purse. Darla caught a glimpse of my Smith & Wesson LadySmith and did a little recoil. I used to carry the S&W Nine, when I was in uniform, a big hunking piece that over the years made my right hip lower than the other. As a PI I went with the more elegant, smaller-frame LadySmith, which still had all the stopping power I ever hoped to need. Naturally, I hoped I'd never need any.

"I'm out of cigarettes. Can I bum one?"

"Sorry, I don't smoke," she said.

Neither do I.

"Guy, you got a cigarette?"

"No, sorry."

So whose cigarette was floating in the toilet?

I sat outside in my car for about an hour, watching the apartment. Nothing was wrong, or everything was wrong, but maybe everything is wrong anyway, half the time. Maybe that's just the way it falls. I sat waiting for Guy to leave, or for Eileen to arrive. I sat thinking about how much I'd like that girl to be not missing and not dead.

9

The first thing they tell you when you move out here is that Pioneer Square was America's original skid row, called Skid Road in those days because the logs from the timber operation on the hill would be sent skidding down Yesler Way to Elliott Bay. Then, Pioneer Square was the gateway to the Yukon, and so many men with broken dreams found themselves marooned there. The bars that gave them solace, the J&M Card Room, Larry's Greenfront, The Central, are still there, but now they charge a joint cover, and on weekends a mob of university students and the suburban young jam the streets to hear local groups and the occasional cowboy band from Montana and to get shit-faced on beer.

All that would start tomorrow night, not that it was entirely dead on a Thursday night. I was tired but too wound up to risk spontaneous combustion alone in my apartment or in my office, so I took a little walk down to Elliott Bay Books.

I negotiated my way past the panhandlers who worked the college kids, ingratiating themselves for a quarter, amusing the kids into turning over some change, God-blessing them if they didn't, as an insult: "God bless you, sir. You have a good night." Translation: Eat shit and die, you little puke! But before that, it's all: "Got a dirty old quarter for a rusty old wino?" "Help out a Gulf War vet?" Like that.

It's their work. Like pigeons, they did what they had to do and they did it loudly and in your face. For the most part, they pissed me off. Still, I usually dropped a quarter on them. Depended on my mood.

A flyer of Eileen looked out at me from behind the bookstore window. I went inside, past the browsers, downstairs to the café, one of my hangouts. I ordered a tall latte and a piece of carrot cake, which is very good there. I hadn't eaten anything since the burrito I'd had for lunch. I sat alone at a table.

Seattle is a city of writers, and some of the tables were taken by those who liked to work in the café, sitting alone with open notebooks or laptops. The walls were lined with hundreds of unjacketed books, not for sale, there only for the ambience and the insulation. Most of those old books, I noticed, were bestsellers of the not-so-distant past, by the giants of that time: Irving Wallace, Harold Robbins, Jacqueline Susann. Disposable stuff that's often recycled but never saved.

As I was scanning the shelves, Vincent appeared at the table.

"Finding anything interesting?"

"I was hoping to find one of your father's."

"May I?"

"You don't have to ask."

He sat down with me.

"The three for tonight: saucer, garage, window," I told him.

He nodded, committing them to memory.

"When I see all these old books," he said, "forgotten or only half remembered, I have to think of my old man. I have to admire the old rascal's perseverance in wresting a living for his family out of the written word, in the midst of so much competition. It couldn't have been easy."

"You're doing it."

"In a way."

"And no one held a gun to his head," I said. "He could have done something else."

"Yes, he could have taken a job at Boeing. He could have properly provided for his family and led a normal life. No assurance that it would have been any better, of course, but at least it would have included health insurance. Not that I have any of that myself."

"Me neither. Stay healthy."

"Oh, I don't worry about not being covered. I sometimes wonder if life in general doesn't involve far too much coverage."

He had his own latte. I offered him a bite of my carrot cake, which he took from the end of my fork. You would have thought we were lovers. I think we wondered, a little, ourselves.

I still had in my inside jacket pocket the small black suede book I had bought, *Scientific Murder Investigation.* I took it out and showed it to Vincent. We went over the list of motives for murder together. God save us, we laughed.

"I got another one," he said. "Mercy. Killing someone to put him out of his misery. I'm just waiting for my father to become miserable enough."

"Maybe Detective May didn't count that as murder."

"The courts do."

"Not in Oregon!"

Detective Luke S. May had been a Seattle homicide cop when Coolidge was president.

He approached a murder case like an architect. You make your plan, you gather your materials, you build your case so that it stands, no matter what blows at it. *Every murder case can be solved.* His italics. Can be but most times isn't. You have to begin, he said, with the question, Who is the victim? To this end he proposed thirty-seven questions that must be answered, including, yes, the usual vital statistics but also the peculiar habits of the deceased, his immediate and future plans, the names and histories of past and current sweethearts, his education, questions of character, his religious beliefs, fraternities or secret societies, et cetera, et cetera. Thirty-seven questions in all.

"Thirty-seven questions would only scratch the surface in my line of work," said Vincent. "Then would come the other questions I have to ask, about his best and worst memories, his pets throughout life, his bowel movements, the size of his graduating class, the size of his *penis.*"

"Now, how could that be a mitigating circumstance?"

"You'd be amazed. Too big, it becomes a weapon, credentials, an imagined skeleton key. Too small, it's a secret, a shame, and overcompensation takes over, not always positive."

Okay, I confess, I haven't seen that many, but I've seen enough. They all looked more or less alike to me. Never found myself scared or disappointed.

"What else?" I asked him.

"I ask about every job he ever held, every doctor he ever saw, every relationship he ever had in life."

"In his *life?*"

"Every single one. I ask how he would use his life if the rest of it were to be spent behind bars. I need to know about any and all drugs, in what amounts, in what combinations, and in whose company. I want to see and have in my file any document ever drawn with the killer's name upon it. All this and more, and how did he sleep and what did he dream about and did he have a favorite song."

Woi Yesus. And I used to wonder about what drew proctologists to that specialty. "You could try your hand at pulp novels, like your father."

"My Friday lunch partner. Hey, Quinn, come with us tomorrow. He'd love to see you again."

"He won't remember me."

"Then he'll enjoy meeting you again. C'mon, keep us company."

"Thing is, I have a job. A case."

"Really?"

"It's okay, isn't it? You don't need me for anything?"

"No, not at the moment. What kind of case?"

"I'm looking for the girl. Eileen Jones."

"Get out."

"Small world, huh? Her boss hired me."

"Arnie whatshisname?"

"Stimick."

"Why would he do that?"

"She's one of four girls he's got working for him. He's the father figure, calls them Arnie's Angels."

"Isn't that nice?"

"Or a little creepy, I haven't decided. Anyway, he's pushed the police and now he's pushing me. The girls are scared and nervous, he's distraught."

"I hope you find her."

"Yeah, everybody does. I talked to her roommate and her boyfriend. Tomorrow morning I'll talk to her mother. The roommate's a little ditzy, the boyfriend looks like your basic slacker. I have the feeling there's something going on between the boyfriend and the roommate." I took a sip of latte, a bite of cake. "I could be wrong."

"It's happened before."

"When?"

He laughed. "You still have to eat lunch."

"What time?"

"Meet me in my office at noon."

"You're a good son."

"I'm just scared. Soon he's going to see me as just another stranger. And me, I really am forgetting far too much. I leave one room and enter another, and I stop cold. I wonder why I left the first one. Opening a drawer, I forget what I'm looking for. Previous addresses gone from my memory. Even the names of old lovers, of dear women who had taken me into their bodies, gone."

He was telling me a tad more than I wanted to know, and he wasn't laughing anymore.

"Relax, some of that happens to everybody," I assured him.

"Yes, I know, but I have a progenitor who can pass on the robber gene that steals all your memories."

"So give me the words."

For a moment he was stymied. "Jeez-Louise, Quinn, I can't remember any of them."

"Relax. Let it come to you. Don't work at it."

"*Saucer?*"

"Score one."

"Something else . . . and *window.*"

"You're on a roll."

"What else? I'm drawing a blank. See what I mean?"

"Two out of three is acceptable. You're all right."

"So we're down for lunch. Maybe by that time the girl will show up and we'll figure out a way for you to take credit for it."

"I got a bad feeling, Vincent, about that girl."

"You always have a bad feeling about something."

"Is that true?"

"You're a pessimist."

"Then why do you hang with me?"

"I'm a realist."

Why that should be the basis for a relationship was left unsaid.

10

Early the next morning I took the ferry to Bainbridge Island to see Eileen's mother, Abby Jones. After the mass of commuters got off the boat, a handful of us walk-ons going in the opposite direction got on it. On the other side an old station wagon taxi took me to her house, four or five miles away on the other side of the island, and down a long gravel driveway off a dead-end country road. The clouds rolled away and we got a little sun break. I was hoping that by the time I got to her house she would tell me that Eileen had called in and all was well.

I didn't have to knock on the door. She must have heard the wheels of the taxi on the gravel, because she was standing in the open doorway, waiting for me to approach. I stopped for just a moment and turned my head up, taking in the sun. What I was hoping for wasn't going to happen.

We wished each other good morning, and I thanked her for agreeing to see me.

"Arnie said it would be a good idea. He wanted to come with you . . ."

"I know. I asked him not to." She was blond, like her daughter, probably of Norwegian descent. A handsome woman, but it looked like she hadn't slept for days. "Are you going through this alone?"

"I talk to my ex in Maui once a day, but there isn't much to say. Arnie tries to help, but what can you do? It's a torture."

I followed her into the house and assured her I would do my best to find her daughter. I didn't tell her that this was my first missing person case.

The house was on the west shore of the island, on a little bay, angled to the northwest, its back to the sun, its face to the south winds and the weather. It was light, all glass on the bay side.

Outside the windows stood three Japanese maples, leafless. A shingled bird feeder hung from one of the naked limbs, for the songbirds. The crows, she told me, bully them when they try to feed. What seeds drop from the feeder are eaten by the waddling ducks that come up from the water. When the crows try to join them, the ducks chase them away. At low tide, the crows try to eat the clams, but there the seagulls chase them away. Crows have no friends in nature. It's just how things worked out.

The bay is called Fletcher Bay, named for an otherwise forgotten early logging contractor who first settled there with his squaw wife. The spit that protects the bay allows for only fifty feet of entry, off the Port Orchard Narrows, and the bay never does get any wider than a dozen good strokes in a kayak, though it runs a nautical mile inland to a small salmon stream. On the charts it is marked as too shallow for navigation. A charming, quiet bay, quite private. I'm not sure I would have traded growing up in the coal regions for the bay, but as a place to wind up, snug harbor, it was hard to beat.

I saw a loom in the far corner of the living room, not quite sure at first what it was. Glass frogs cluttered the mantel. I could smell the salt water. I could hear some geese.

We sat in the breakfast nook and had tea and oatmeal cookies, baked by her. I used to do that, when Nelson was still at home. Anymore, I don't bake cookies. I don't bake anything anymore.

Abby was the kind of girl would cut a hamburger in half, even though she was going to eat both halves anyway. She was the kind who would never invite me to a party unless my husband was coming, too. Women like her often suspected I was a lesbian. Not that some men didn't think the same. For the record, I'm not, though once I wondered hard what I would look for in a woman, if I ever decided to take the plunge, so to speak. I decided that I would look for the same qualities in a woman as I would in a man, so why bother, except that the chances of finding those qualities were way better if you're looking for women.

I tried to give her a chance to start the conversation, to volunteer something.

"I had to do something . . . so I baked cookies," she said. "I'm trying to keep myself occupied."

"I know," I said, but I could only guess. "Has Eileen ever gone away anywhere without telling you?"

"No, never. She doesn't call me every day, but she always calls if she's going somewhere."

"Like where?"

"Oh, skiing, or to the gorge for a concert, or to Vancouver for the weekend."

"Did she go to Canada often? Did she know anybody up there?"

"I don't think so. She went a couple of

times with Darla, and I think once with Guy."

"Any particular reason?"

"No, just for the good exchange rate and a weekend away."

"How long has she been seeing Guy?"

"Three . . . four months."

"That's okay with you?"

"Not entirely, but I keep quiet about it. You said you met him . . . and Darla?"

"Last night. I have a son, so I can't say, but on first sight I probably wouldn't be too thrilled to have my daughter bring him home."

"She didn't bring him home. I met him with her in Seattle, for coffee, where he works. We had only the briefest conversation. He's all right, I'm sure, but not exactly a mother's dream. I just figured it would run its course. I dated some losers in my day, too."

"So did we all, ain't? Did she ever talk about any people she didn't like, who didn't like her?"

"Everybody likes Eileen. She's a very positive person, giving and thoughtful. People like being around her."

"Whoa!"

"What?"

"Just saw a fish rising. Good size, nice splash."

"We have a salmon run in the fall, to the spawning creek at the end of the bay. But during the year there's always the rogue salmon that comes in here to explore. I've caught a few right off my dock."

"Eileen must have loved growing up here."

"She couldn't wait to get off the island. Most of the young people can't wait. But I've seen them years later, trying to come back. I couldn't be anywhere else but right here on the bay."

"Did she like her boss, Arnie Stimick?"

"I think so. She never said otherwise. She said he was very generous to them, the girls. Twice a month he would take them all out to a nice dinner. Often he would get tickets, complimentary tickets to shows and games and things, and he would pass them on to Eileen and the other girls. I met him once or twice. He was always very gracious to me."

"Did you ever meet anyone else in the building, where Eileen works?"

"No, just Arnie and the other girls."

"Did she ever mention a Bernard, who has an office there?"

"Bernard? No. Wait a minute. When we were leaving the building we passed a young black man getting out of the elevator. Eileen said hello to him and I believe she called him Bernard. She didn't introduce us, it was just a quick passing. I didn't ask about him. Why?"

"Just trying to ascertain who she knew there. You've called her on her cell phone?"

"Almost hourly. It goes right to message."

"And the police have checked her phone records?"

"Yes. The last call she made was during her lunch break, to Guy."

I went ahead and looked at her room. Over the last several months Abby had been encroaching into it with weaving materials and clear cases full of arts and crafts stuff. I did the same thing once I realized that Nelson would be returning infrequently.

"Do you know what brand of cigarettes she smoked?"

"Cigarettes?"

"Yes, were they filter-tipped?"

"Eileen doesn't smoke."

"She doesn't?"

"No." She seemed surprised I would ask.

I asked her a few more questions, then said I'd better call the taxi. She insisted on driving me to the ferry landing, and so we spent another ten minutes talking, but none

of it was getting me any closer to her daughter.

11

"Beer, hat, and summer."

This time it was Vincent giving me the three new words, on our way to pick up his father at the rest home. I humored him. I could remember three random words for days, years maybe.

Vincent had a standing Friday date with his dad, Clinton, who was the last remnant of his family, since Vincent had never married and had no children, or so I thought at the time. Sometimes I went with them. Everybody's got to eat, and to tell you the truth I got a kick out of the old coot.

In fact, I enjoyed the lunches more than Vincent did, and his dad never liked them all that much, either, though it was hard to know what Clinton thought about anything or how much he enjoyed any particular moment. He was living in the Olympic Wing of the rest home, a light care unit, one of only a few Alzheimer's patients housed there. If he survived long enough, he would eventually be transferred to the Cascade Wing, lockup, with the more advanced demential residents. An electronic bracelet kept him from wandering too far away. He was ambulatory, with the aid of a cane he named Mabel. He roamed the hallways like a ghost while others sat in their wheelchairs or stayed in their rooms. Clinton, that frail old man on his last legs, with little of his mind left, would turn out to be very important to this story. You never know, ain't?

We walked through the lobby and into the main corridor and found him poised on the edge of a chair outside the dining room. He was sitting next to his only friend, Howard the Magnificent, a retired and widowed barber who, as far as I know, never did anything remarkable during his life. Unless it was reaching such an advanced age. Maybe he dreamed of being a professional wrestler. Watching wrestling on television was a favorite pastime at the home.

Clinton didn't recognize us for a few moments. Then he struggled to his feet and Vincent gave him a loose hug.

"Did they tell you I was here?" he asked, which is the kind of question Alzheimer's people ask.

"Go get Mabel, Dad. We're taking you to lunch."

Clint looked around. He'd lost his cane. Howard the Magnificent had to tell him he'd left it in his room. Vincent was going to get it for him, but the old man insisted he had to do it, because Mabel was hiding. So off he went, gripping the handrail along the wall, making his way to his room. Sometimes he even forgets he has a room. He forgets where it's located in the world. Vincent gave him a head start, then followed to make sure he'd come back.

I waited with Howard the Magnificent.

"Who're you?" he asked.

"The name's Quinn."

"That old man had a crying jag this morning."

"Clinton?" I was surprised. He was a tough old nut. "Why was he crying?"

"*E.T.* was the movie this morning, and when little E.T. said, 'I want to go home,' well, that started the waterworks. We all want to go home, but we know we never will. Next stop, the boneyard."

Clinton, in his day, was a writer of pulp novels. They were described as hard-boiled, two-fisted. Now he weeps at the movies.

His books were paperback originals: hard-boiled mysteries, westerns, sea adventures.

His audiences were tough guys with short attention spans and limited vocabularies. The novels sold well enough to support a family, if he could churn out ten a year, which he did, year in and year out. Over his lifetime he wrote hundreds of them, under several different novelty pen names. Pete Moss, Lee Ward, Buster de Pared, among others. Four of his novels were optioned by the movies, for what seemed at the time princely sums. The money was quickly squandered on bad investments: crabbing boats, low-lying real estate, experimental fiction quarterlies. None of the proposed movies was ever actually produced. Vincent managed his expenses out of the equity from the sale of his house in Ballard.

We drove to the restaurant in Vincent's Isuzu Trooper, a treacherous little rig. Clinton was cinched into it with his cane under the chest harness, which could break him in half should we have a head-on collision.

"Where are you taking me?"

"The Beeliner Diner."

"I don't believe I've ever been there."

"You have, you just don't remember."

It was the place they had been going to every week for the past year, eating exactly the same thing, and Clinton not remembering a bit of it by the time they got back to the nursing home. Vincent chose it originally because he thought it would stimulate his father. What's more, the food was cheap and delicious. The two big-busted professional waitresses thought it was sweet that every Friday, Vincent brought his old dad to lunch, and sometimes me, and what they made of me I don't know.

People were lined up waiting for tables, which was usually the case, so when three seats at the counter opened up we grabbed them.

The printed motto of the place was, EAT IT AND BEAT IT. The waitresses, Ruth Ann and Angela, were loud and friendly. The music was just loud.

"This is some place," Clint observed, not for the first time.

"I bet in your day you spent a lot of time in joints like this," I said.

"Yeah."

"Researching atmosphere for your books and stuff," I prompted, hoping it would spur a memory.

"We'd better get back now. It's getting late."

"We just got here, Dad," Vincent said. "Aren't you hungry?"

He said that, yes, he could eat a little

something.

Clinton looked at the menu as though it were an ink-blot test. He would study the menu throughout the meal, reading aloud.

"What do you feel like eating today?" Vincent asked him.

"Oh, I don't know. It all looks bad."

"You always like the charcoal-broiled pork chops."

"Pork chops? *Pork* chops?" he said, like he was some kind of Orthodox Jew. "You gotta be kidding."

"Charbroiled."

"Okay, I'll give them a try."

Truth was, Vincent told me, he had the pork chops every Friday, with potato pancakes and applesauce, and disappointing coffee. Never a change, week after week. And every time, half an hour later, with his failing body working hard at digesting it, he could not remember what he ate. Vincent always wondered where it went, burned probably in the exhausting fight to hold on to memories.

"I met with the mother this morning," I told Vincent, Clint still deep into the menu.

"How did that go?"

"Okay, I guess. Said her daughter wouldn't take off without calling, et cetera. Had no enemies, boyfriend is flaky and maybe cheating on her, but the girl doesn't seem like anybody's targeted victim."

"So if something did happen to her, it was probably random."

"Lord knows that's happened before."

"Sad and unexplainable."

"Listen, that story you told me about meeting her that time at the FedEx kiosk . . ."

"Yes?"

"Are you sure she was smoking?"

"Of course I am. That's what started the conversation."

"Because her mother said she didn't smoke."

"Probably she just never told her mother she did."

"Yeah, but smokers, you can smell it on them."

"She was smoking."

"You remember the brand? Filter tip or reg?"

"How would I know that?"

"I guess you wouldn't. Thing is, yesterday, when I visited her apartment? I found a filter tip floating in the toilet."

"There were people there, though, right?"

"Yeah. Her roommate and her boyfriend. Only they said they didn't smoke, either."

"Odd."

"A little. Part of me wanted to think Eileen was there. I wanted to think she was in the bathroom smoking a cigarette when I knocked on the door, and she dumped it and hid in a closet."

"Why?"

"Because she's supposed to be missing."

"Does that make sense?"

"Not a lot. But there's a lot I don't know."

Though frail, Clinton wasn't in such bad shape, physically. He would probably live long enough so that someone would have to take over the task of spooning food into his mouth and wiping his behind. Was there any pleasure left in his life, any purpose? Everything was either too noisy or too quiet, too lonely or too crowded, too long or too short. On the other hand, what the hell, he was alive, in the world in some fashion, like everyone else, and why should he not stay, playing at survival just like the rest of us, even though we know that the game is lost from the very beginning.

I may not be the best detective in the world — I'm third-string at most — but I have good instincts, and I sensed that Vincent and his old dad were on a strange collision course.

Vincent ordered for both of them. I was going to have clam chowder and salad.

The waitress poured Clinton's coffee, saying, "I made sure you didn't get the last cup in the pot."

He looked at her blankly.

"You always complain the last cup is bitter," Vincent reminded him.

"The hell. I never complain about anything. What good would it do?" He sipped the coffee and said, "It's not hot. Everybody knows, except these lunkheads, that coffee ought to be served hot."

"The cup itself was cold, I'll bet. Your second cupful will stay warm."

His dad read aloud from the menu. "Chicken-fried steak with mashed potatoes and gravy. Taco salad. Tuna melt . . ."

Vincent let him read on. Why try to stop him? Everything they had done or said since coming into the Beeliner Diner, they had done and said every Friday afternoon since they'd been conducting this father-son ritual, like a feverish dream.

"So what do you do now?" he asked me.

"I'll stop in and see if the police will talk to me. May have to get the local press to run with it. Arnie could help with that. Apparently, he has connections. Eileen's young, white, and pretty, I'm kind of surprised the press isn't already over it. They don't see a story yet, I guess. Did you know

Bernard knew her?"

"Bernard did?"

"Maybe like you knew her, but he thinks she had the hots for him."

"Really? What makes him think that?"

"God knows. His street name was Romeo, so maybe it's put a burden on him."

"Bernard has left the streets for good, and I can see the streets leaving him, too. He's like a regular guy now."

"I could go back and see the lady on the island, but I'm embarrassed to go back with nothing."

"At night," Clinton said, "a lady comes into my room."

"I wish I could say the same," said Vincent.

"She scares me."

"Women scare me, too. Should we blame Mom?"

Sometimes Vincent has a little fun with him, like that, just to break the monotony. He doesn't know the difference.

"She reads to me out of a book."

"What book?"

"I don't know. A book."

"Could be a volunteer," I said, "come in and read the old folks to sleep."

"Do you like that?" Vincent asked him.

"I don't want to hurt her feelings."

"That's nice. You know, you never used to care about others' feelings, so in some ways things are getting better."

"Aw, shaddup."

"Or maybe not."

"Sometimes she has a smoke while she's reading."

"What? They're not supposed to do that. I'm going to have a talk with the staff. That's just outrageous, smoking in an old person's room."

Vincent excused himself and went to the men's room.

"Meat loaf . . . pork loin . . . fish-and-chips . . . ," his father read aloud.

"Who were you when you lived before," I asked him, not putting too fine a point on it, not even looking at him. It's something I do, with old people losing touch with this world, and especially with toddlers. Try it yourself, just when they get to putting words together, before they buy into the current reality. Ask them, What was it like when you were big? Don't be surprised if they tell you.

This is what Clinton told me: "A happier person in a better place. It was warmer there."

"Where?"

"By the river."

"What did you do?"

98

"I sewed. Sewed up clothes for people."

This was good. I was getting excited. It's not like something I believe in; it's something I accept, like gravity. Once I saw the proof of it, that time when Odd and I made our discovery. After that, I kept recognizing it where other people might not. I asked Clinton who he'd lived with then, but I had already lost him. All he said was, "Chicken wings . . . potato skins . . ."

Vincent came back and sat down. He looked at his father and saw that he was off in the endless corridors of his own mind.

"I wonder how much I'll remember," he said. "Will I even remember that once I had a father. He doesn't. I might not even remember all the lives I've saved. The scab on my knee might ultimately be more engaging than anything else that ever happened in my long life."

"So?"

"Huh?"

"So what's wrong with that? The scab on your knee might be at the moment the most interesting thing around."

"Quinn, sometimes I wonder why I confide in you."

"Sometimes I wonder myself. You know I take notes."

"Thanks for reminding me. Now give me

the three little words."

"Beer, hat, summer," I shot back.

He didn't say anything. "Well?"

"I don't know if you're right or not. I already forgot them."

I laughed . . . alone.

"Dad? Did Quinn tell you? Something bad has happened. A girl who works in our building? Two floors above? She's missing. Everybody's worried she may have, you know, been attacked or something."

And what did the old man say to that? "Hangtown fry . . . spaghetti and meatballs . . . chef's salad . . ."

Vincent turned back to me. "A missing girl is the sort of lurid news that he once thrived upon."

"Well, that was then."

"When I was a social worker, right out of U-Dub, he used to pump me for details about the wretchedness of my caseload. He would then use my clients for his stories, with little or no disguise, except for the emphasis on the underbelly."

"Now it's all underbelly," I said.

The old man was bobbing his head. Of course it's possible he was only keeping time with the Gypsy Kings, no easy deal for a nonmusician.

"She's only eighteen," Vincent told the old

man. "So pretty, such a glow of youth." He seemed to have an aching heart about it.

"Who?"

"The missing girl. Eileen."

"Do you know her?"

"Kind of. Not really. But she's popular in the building. Everybody is really upset, because . . . you know . . . they fear the worst."

"The worst what?"

"He's an old man with Alzheimer's," I said. "Give him a break. He doesn't know what you're talking about."

"A girl comes into my room at night," said Clinton.

Vincent looked uneasy, maybe ill. I asked him what was wrong.

"A sense of deep dread is unfolding inside of me, Quinn."

"Could be a potassium deprivation," I said. "Have a glass of orange juice."

I was kidding a little, but he called for one anyway. He drank it right down. By that time our food had come.

"Did that help?"

"Not a bit. You know what's bothering me?"

"Should I ask?"

"If Eileen turns up murdered, and if her killer is arrested, you know I'll be getting the call."

"You da man."

"And, granted, the connection between me and Eileen is slim, practically non-existent, but it's there: I spoke to her. She was beguiling. We had a moment together. It affected me, I don't know."

"Look, even if she was murdered, they may never find her. If they do find her, they might never find the killer. So stop anticipating."

He went all dreamy on me.

He wiped the applesauce from his dad's mouth. Infancy to infancy, I thought. Conversation in flashes, often in questions unanswerable or requiring a lie, temper tantrums, sullenness, boredom the enemy, with no resources to fight back. No more reading beyond menu items. Even TV required more concentration than the old man could muster. Count the change in your pocket, over and over, play with the coins. Afraid of the dark.

12

Me, sitting one bench up from the three Indians, all of us out of the drizzle, under the pergola. They're panhandling, but they're not much better at that job than at any other. Booze has taken away their will to work, to love, to live. They make their pitches from the bench, so anyone who gives them anything has to really want to give them something. The marks have to get off the sidewalk, walk the few steps over cobblestones, and drop something into the overturned caps. Nobody does, as far as I can see.

Turning my head to the left, I can take in the Pioneer Building, my building. Across the street I can see my apartment building. And splitting James and Yesler like a ship plowing through the sea is the parking lot. I can see the movement of cars, leaving for the day, and some movement of people going to them, but not much else. Someone could be being attacked and I wouldn't know it.

I see Bernard leave the building from the side door and cross in the middle of the street to the parking lot. In a few minutes I see his car, a black Mustang. I see a number of people vaguely familiar to me take the same path. I see their cars leave and turn down Second. Some I know leave by the front door, walking uptown, downtown, across the street. And here comes Arnie, with his three remaining Angels. Two of them walk behind my back to the bus stop. I can turn my head to the right and watch them until they reach it, just as Arnie is watching them. He waves to them, once they are safe at the bus stop, and escorts the remaining girl across the street, again in the middle, which in Seattle is a ticket usually enforced. There isn't much advantage in crossing that way anyhow, because you can't enter the lot unless you go up to Second. Arnie and the girl walk the other way, around the point of the lot, up Yesler to the entrance on that side, which does save you half a block's walk. They disappear from my view, but then in a moment I can see Arnie get into his car, a Range Rover, nice green color. I can't see the girl so I'm guessing she's safe in her own car because Arnie is alone in his.

I'm watching all that. And I lose an Indian, not that they were mine to mind. I see him staggering up Yesler. He crosses to the lot. In a few minutes he returns, and I know he was there for a piss. Sometimes they go in my alley. It stinks there.

Then I see Vincent, leaving by the side door. My impulse is to call out to him, but I don't. I don't know why exactly. I'm content just to watch. I don't feel like talking. Unlike the Indians, who can't stop. They talk about salmon and other fish. Clams and oysters enter the conversation. Then crabs, the real money fish, the fish men die for. Vincent crosses in the middle and then crosses again to the alley, disappearing into it. Why would he go home via the underground parking? In a few minutes I see his Trooper come out of the alley and turn up Yesler, so that makes sense to me, though I have to wonder where he's going.

I sit there for the better part of an hour, until the foot traffic and the car traffic slowly diminish.

Last Tuesday, Eileen Jones was one of those many people, crossing in the middle or crossing at the crosswalk. She either got into her car and drove away, to an unknown place for an unknown reason, or she was attacked in that parking lot and taken away in her own car. I shudder involuntarily.

■ ■ ■ ■

PART TWO

■ ■ ■ ■

1

I don't always test Vincent with three little words, not every time I see him. I didn't when I went to tell him they found Eileen's body.

We were in his office, me sitting on his wicker chair, warming my hands around a latte.

"She was found by a Guatemalan woman named Concepción," I told him.

The poor lady was working off her community service hours for being caught in an exception to her constitutional right to the pursuit of happiness. Weed.

She screamed *Jesus!* It came out *Hay-sus! Hay-sus! Hay-sus!* First she dropped the bag, then she tossed the prong. She ran like she never ran before, through standing water on the shoulder of Route 509, just north of Burien, cars splashing her with chilly water, drenching her. *Hay-sus! Hay-sus! Hay-sus!*

"A minute earlier she was stabbing Mc-Donald's paper cups and stuffing them in her trash bag, cursing in Spanish the rain and the traffic splashing her. The guy told me, she stopped to pick up a thrown hubcap and she didn't want to weigh down her bag so she flung it down into the brush. She's watching its flight, you know, the way you do, and . . . there's a body. The raincoat and the skirt bunched up at the thighs. *Hay-sus!* The supervisor had to hold her, give her a chance to catch her breath. She doesn't know much English but she knew how to say *dead body.*"

Vincent rolled his black Tombow roller-ball between his fingers, his elbows on the desk.

"Stimick's distraught. He sent his girls home, closed up shop. Everybody's taking it pretty hard. My guess is, she left the building, went across the street to the parking lot, and somebody grabbed her and took her in her own car."

"Across the street? James Street?"

"Yeah, looks like. The car's still missing."

"That's a busy corner."

"Pretty busy. That time of evening."

"Someone would have seen it."

"People are trying to make it to their own cars, looking out for themselves. He could

110

have come up behind her, put a knife to her neck or a gun to her head and forced her in the car. After that, who knows? I don't have a lot of details, but I picked up that there was no blood. Cause of death still to be determined. All I know is the asshole pulls to the side of the road and dumps her over the embankment in the dark."

"No suspects?"

"No. It looks random. The only way to get him now is the car."

Vincent let out a long breath, pulled on his beard. "And nobody's seen the car, I guess."

"No, not yet."

The phone rang. Vincent let it ring a few times, but I knew he would answer it. He listened for less than a minute and pursed his lips. All he said was okay and he hung up.

"Jon Kutzmann's lawyer. The jury came in with a guilty verdict."

"Yeah, well, big surprise. Glad they did."

"It was a slam dunk. I guess I better call his aunt, give it one more try."

"Why don't you go see her, have a face-to-face. You need to get out of here for a while. I'll drive you there."

He went along with it and I drove him to North Bend in my PT Cruiser, a divorce gift to myself. I had the time. I was out of a job now. I hated that I wasn't able to find her alive, but the truth was that she was dead before I was ever hired to find her.

We went up to the front door of the small tract house and I gave it a few hard raps. Vincent was still a little preoccupied.

When she opened the door, Vincent said, "Mrs. Chelmsford, I'm Vincent Ainge."

"Who?"

"I'm the one who's been calling you? About your nephew, Jon?"

"Jesus, not again."

"And you know my assistant, Quinn."

She gave me a sideways glance. I wasn't all that thrilled to see her again, either.

"I told you everything already," she whined.

"Yes, I know —"

"They found him guilty today," I blurted out. So call me insensitive.

Even though she had expected it as much as we did, the reality shook her for a moment. Then she sighed, as only sad old people can, and she said, "What else could they do?"

"It looks very bad for Jon," said Vincent.

"He murdered two little boys!"

"Yes, that's true."

"What are you supposed to do with a

grown man who murders two little boys?"

"Jon wasn't born a murderer. You, of all people, must know that."

She wasn't quick to back him up.

"Don't you?"

"No, sir, I'm not sure I do know that. Only God knows that."

"Would God even let a murderer be born?"

"He does things His own way, God."

"Yes, ma'am, so God should continue with His mysterious plan, whatever that may be, don't you agree?"

Vincent no more believed in a grand plan than he believed in the Deity. Vincent believed we were on our own here. We could make it a little better or we could make it a lot worse. On that much, I was with him. Me, I know death doesn't end it, it just flips it. Who or what is behind all that is beyond me. But Vincent works with whatever presents itself. Right now, it was God, and he'd make Him an ally. To God-fearing folk, Vincent liked to point out that the state should not do what only God has the right to do.

"I can't help Jon anymore."

"No, that's not true. There's a lot you can do. You can testify. You might say the one right sentence that can save his life. That's all it takes, you know, the one right sentence. Sometimes only three little words."

"I don't have any notion what you're talking about."

"You can provide some answers about Jon. That's what I'm talking about."

"Answers? How can anybody make excuses for why a grown man would do such things to little helpless boys? There's no answer for that. Jon's gone down a dark, dark road, that's all. Somewhere along the way he just turned bad like something that shoulda been brought inside."

"Yes! That's it, exactly! That's what I'm after. Had he only been brought inside, huh? Why did he go bad, and should he hang because of it? If a man can turn bad, he can always turn good again."

"You don't believe that, Mr. Ainge, and neither do I."

"I would like to believe it. He's a bad man, Mrs. Chelmsford, we can agree on that. I don't know how he got that way, but it wasn't by the touch of God. Or Satan. *People* did that to him. He is blood of your blood, flesh of your flesh, and once you loved him. I don't want him ever set free. No, I want bars between him and the rest of the world for as long as he lives, but what sense does it make to hang Jon by the neck until he's dead? I don't want that as part of the world I live in, and I don't think you do, either."

She backed into the house and started to close the door on us.

"Let's go, Vincent," I said, but he wasn't willing to give it up.

"Mrs. Chelmsford, please." She paused, the door still open a head's width. "Mrs. Chelmsford, faceless people are going to hang your nephew. Your sister's child. His neck is going to break, if he's lucky, or he's going to strangle on his own tongue if he's not. And excuse me, but when they bring his body out of Walla Walla in a box, there will be only two kinds of people in your family. Those who tried to stop it and those who stood by and did nothing."

She looked at us for a long moment, half safe in her house, half exposed to this passion of a stranger. It was as passionate as Vincent ever got. Even I was a little taken back.

"You seem like a nice young man. You must have your own life to lead."

"Thank you. That's what I'm doing. This is my life."

"I have been hiding away in shame."

"I understand."

At last she said, "Would you like to come inside out of the rain? I got coffee on."

2

I pulled the PT into my parking slot in the underground below the apartments. Instead of taking the elevator, we both went up the ramp to the alley, held our noses, and walked through the wino jamboree to Yesler and then across the street to the Pioneer Building.

The pederast's old auntie was in the bag — Vincent had persuaded her to testify at the penalty phase — and he looked a little better for it. We didn't talk any more about Eileen. I knew Vincent was dreading the part he might have to play in all this. If and when the killer was found, he would be obliged to try to save his life. Me, I was more worried that no killer would ever be found, especially if it had been a random murder, which seemed to be the case. Motive: for the hell of it.

Vincent went off to his office, and I let him believe I was going off to mine, but I stayed on the elevator to the sixth floor. I tried Stimick's door. It was open.

I knew he'd sent his phone girls home when the bad news came in, but I was halfway sure he didn't have much of a home to go to or people to be with.

The door to his office was two inches ajar and I could hear him sobbing into his hands. I moved sideways a little. They call us gumshoes for a reason. Mine are black Rockports and they don't make a sound. I saw him through the crack, his head bent over his desk, a big automatic in his hands, looked like a 9. Whoa. Was I here in the nick of time or what?

A skinny dude with long hair and a MY MOMMA LIVES IN BAKERSFIELD T-shirt, you expect to see crying once in a while, but a balding, bulky six-foot-fiver, sitting alone at his office desk, it's a little more unsettling. Either way, I'm a woman and it's in my code, I got to say, There, there, it'll be all right. It may be in my code, and occasionally I'll give it a shot, but I'm terrible at it.

I pushed the door and widened the opening. The movement startled him. His head snapped up. And then the nine-millimeter was leveled at me, making unfriendly gestures.

"Whoa!" said I, my hands up. "Goddam-mit!"

Da frick.

"Sorry, Quinn. Didn't mean to scare you."

"You're still scaring me."

He put the gun into a drawer. I dropped my hands and started breathing again.

He grabbed a tissue and filled it with snot. He dropped it into the wastebasket. Holding his mud was a major struggle.

"I thought you might still be here," I said.

"I wasn't until half an hour ago. I went over on the ferry to be with Abby, Eileen's mother."

"How is she?"

"I had to call a doctor, have her sedated. Everybody knows her so I was able to . . . I talked her into letting me identify the body. Officially. There's no doubt it's her."

"You've done that already?"

"No, I'm getting ready to. I should be there by now."

"You want me to come with you?"

"No . . . thanks. I wanted Abby to always remember Eileen as she was, alive, smiling. No mother should have to . . ."

"You're right."

"She was so . . . winning," he said. "Positive. Optimistic. Everything to live for . . ."

He lifted a small framed photograph and

turned it toward me. Eileen. I scanned his desk for others but there were none: no wife, no kids, no dog, no Corvette, even.

"Look at this face."

"It's a sad day," I said, stating the obvious, which works so well with some people during times of grief. He nodded. I looked at the bookcase along the side wall and saw three more framed photographs. The other girls.

"She had some sense of humor," he said. "So open and friendly."

"I heard that."

"Too friendly. Too open."

"It would seem."

" 'My Funny Valentine,' I called her."

"What did you call the others?"

"What others?"

"The other girls," I said, nodding toward the pictures.

"Arnie's Angels."

"Yeah, I forgot." I took one of the pictures off the shelf. "What did you call this one?"

"That's Claire. The Monitor. She doesn't let you get away with anything."

I had a boss, this lieutenant — hell knows what he called me — if my body turned up, he'd have a Bushmills, say, "Tragic thing," and call it a day. Arnie Stimick, it seemed, just had some interior spaces condemned for occupancy when Eileen went missing and turned up dead. I could sit with him for the rest of the day and still not finger his freak out of a lineup of five. Whatever she represented to him, it was gone now, for good.

"Listen," I said, "you don't owe me anything. I was only on it a few days and I got nowhere, so . . ."

"That's decent of you."

"Well, under the circumstances . . ."

"But I would like to keep you on retainer."

"Really? Why?"

"Find out who murdered her, Quinn. Get the son of a bitch who murdered my girl."

"Every cop in King County is on it as we speak. I'd only get in the way."

"No, that's not true. You're smart, you got good instincts. I'll put in a call or two and make sure you have access to everything the police have. You ever find a murderer before?"

"Once. But it took me a lifetime, in a manner of speaking."

He raised his eyebrows but had no real curiosity about anything else I might have done. He wanted me to do this. I made one more halfhearted attempt to tell him to save his money, but in the end I told him I'd do my best. He nodded. Good enough.

3

Arnie was true to his word. Sergeant Beck-man, though not without some reluctance, opened up the murder book to me. It was thin. Since Eileen's car was still missing, the only direct and hard evidence to examine was the scene of the crime and the body itself. The body had been dumped right off Route 509, in a section where some traffic might be expected in the early evening. The scenario I liked was that someone had grabbed her in the parking lot, wanted her car or her or both. He either killed her right there in the parking lot or pushed her into the car still alive. He had to do the driving. But if she was alive, why would she sit still for it? Maybe she was too open, too trust-ing. Maybe she thought quiet cooperation would end with her safely standing on the street watching her car go away. Did he kill her while driving the car down the road? Like, how? Because, and this really interested me, there was no blood on the body. The exact cause of death was still to be determined, but eyeballing told them that the means of death was not a gun, knife, or blunt instrument. If he did kill her in the parking lot and put the body in the car and dump it during his getaway, early during the get-away, then he pulled to the side in rush-hour traffic. Pulled to the side and pulled her out of the car and rolled her down the embankment in the headlights of God-knows-how-many cars heading home for dinner. Not out of the realm. It might even be easier to go unnoticed during rush hour than in the middle of the night, when one solitary car might take an interest in another parked by the side. During rush hour a hundred cars jockeying for lane position might drive by without ever seeing something off the shoulder.

How did he kill her in the first place? Break her neck? Suffocate her? Ether, poison, heroin? All seemed unlikely if my random-attack scenario was true. Of course, it could have been someone she knew. Most murders are that way. Either case, she could have been killed in another place at another time and just dumped where she was, but I couldn't believe that anyone other than a first-time killer in the midst of a panic would choose to drop his victim by the side of the road.

So for the moment, without becoming wed to the idea, I was going to go with a man, known or unknown to Eileen, crushing, choking, or otherwise subduing her, then realizing what he had done, panicking, and getting rid of the body at the first opportunity. Now, what did he do with her car? And with her purse? Were there cigarettes in that purse? Were there birth control pills?

While waiting and hoping for those questions to be answered, I thought I'd go up to Belltown and get a latte at Starbucks. Something, I knew, was not quite right with the boyfriend Guy. And the roommate Darla. Or both of them together.

Guy wasn't the espresso jerk on duty. He'd gone home, they told me, when he got the word. They wouldn't give me his home address. I got that from Darla, who also went home from work as soon as she heard her friend was dead. I could have gone to see her, but I had more interest in the boy.

Just as Magnolia is as far north as a young person wants to be away from downtown, Georgetown is as far south. Any farther, you might as well be in Kent, Seattle's punch line. Unlike Magnolia, however, Georgetown was hip, the last cool place to find cheap rents, refuge for artists of all stripes.

Buffeted from Interstate 5 by the old Rainier brewery, which was being parceled into artists' lofts, Georgetown lay low and inconspicuous, slow to give up its blue-collar industrial façade despite the boutique galleries cropping up. Guy's place, half a crumbling duplex, was on a dead-end street behind a Vespa repair shop.

The door was answered by a young man whose pants ended just below his knees, the better to display his tattoos, which circled his calves like a sideshow. I was looking at the tats because his face was too hard to dwell on, given the studs and rings sprouting and dangling from his chin, his lips, his nose, his ears, and the outside corners of both baby blues. His tongue, too, I discovered when he opened his mouth.

"I'm looking for Guy," I said.

"Oh, this is where he lives, but he's not here now. Is there something I can help you with?"

The walking diorama was polite and articulate and possibly gay.

"It's about his girlfriend."

"Oh, yes. God. Horrible. Crazy horrible."

"Do you know where he is?"

"No. He came home and packed a bag

and hopped on his bike."

"Motorcycle, right?"

"Yes, a Kawasaki. Crotch rocket. It can go a hundred and seventy miles an hour. He's gone a hundred and twenty on it, he says."

"Yeah, well, I'm not so much interested in his ride as I am in where the hell he's gone."

"May I ask, who are you?"

"Detective. Private type."

I gave him my card.

"Oh. Okay. Well, Guy was just wiped out, destroyed by all this. He had to get away, he said."

"Did he say where?"

"No. Just that he had to get away."

"You have his phone number?"

"You mean his mobile? No, I never call him, except maybe here."

"You the only roommate?"

"No, there's Jeff. He sculpts. He has a studio not far from here."

"Does Jeff know his cell number?"

"I doubt it. You can ask him. We're not all that close, the three of us. We just share the rent. You don't think Guy had anything to do with . . . ?"

"I'd feel better about it if he hadn't taken it on the arfy-darfy so quick."

"The what?"

"I wish he hadn't run away."

126

"I don't think he did. I mean, not permanently. He's just . . . overcome. He's done it before, you know, when things get too heavy on him, he hops on the bike and motors somewhere. He always comes back in a day or two."

"And when he does, does he tell you where he's been?"

"Vancouver is one place."

"Washington or Canada?"

"Canada. On that bike it takes him about two hours."

"Will you tell him to call me, if he checks in, or when he comes back?"

"I'll be happy to."

"And maybe get his number?"

"I could ask."

"You ever hear him talk on that phone?"

"Sure, now and again."

"Like, who, for instance?"

"Oh, Darla . . ."

"Darla?"

"Or Eileen, I get them mixed up."

"So you never partied with them? Or Jeff?"

"No. Not unless I ran into them somewhere."

"So you didn't really know Eileen?"

"No . . ."

"Or Darla?"

". . . just to say hello."

I worried about Guy zooming away to Canada on the day his girlfriend was found dead, but as it worked out I didn't have to worry for long.

4

The funeral was that Friday. Arnie arranged for a bus to pick us up on the island side and take us to the church. Forty or so of us took the walk from the building to the Coleman Dock and got on board the ferry.

We had coffee, read the paper, made some small talk. I briefed Arnie on my progress, or lack of it. I told him about Guy doing an Easy Rider, and I told him that the cause of Eileen's death was suffocation, likely the result of a choke hold held too long. Time of death uncertain. He sat quietly, nodding his head to everything I said.

On the island, we boarded the bus for the short ride to St. Cecilia's. It took all of five minutes, and during those minutes I scanned the faces of the passengers. Any one of them could be the killer. It could be Bernard, sitting right next to me. It could be the architect I met in the elevator, sitting near the rear, or Arnie, sitting behind the driver, or one of his girls, one next to him, the other two behind him, though I doubted they had that kind of choke hold, or the computer geek from the third floor, whose holds I also doubted, or . . . hell, it could have been anybody. We all sat in silence.

Vincent wanted to come, but I talked him out of it. Take your father to lunch, I told him, I'll make your apologies. Neither one of us wanted to talk about why he shouldn't be there. His job is hard enough, saving those who kill from being killed in retribution. It required not dwelling on the victim or on the crime, cold as that might seem.

We stepped off the bus into a light drizzle. Most of us went right into the church, but I chose to stay outside and study who showed up.

Guy, as far as I knew, was still in Canada. At least he'd never called me back. I was considering spending a day across the border trying to track him down when guess who showed up? He held Darla's arm. He wore shades and a corduroy sport coat, borrowed was my guess, and a tie of uncertain vintage. He was doing his best, and I felt a little better about him. I didn't stop them as they headed for the church door, and they didn't notice me. I'd talk to them both later.

A crowd was bottlenecking at the entrance

and I was about to join them when I saw Vincent's Isuzu pull into the lot. He got out and ran around the car to open the door for his father. I was not happy to see them.

"What are you doing here? Da frick."

"Dad, you remember Quinn?"

"Quinn? What kind of name is that for a woman?"

"We had lunch on the ferry," Vincent told me.

The old man was wearing a rugged gray Pendleton with leather patches on the elbow. He looked like a professor emeritus.

"Nice jacket," I said to Clinton, who was transfixed by a stained-glass window.

"I forgot he had it. I found it in his closet. God, Quinn, his roommate is dying. They've got the room draped in darkness. To ease his passing. Does that work? We're not born into darkness, why would we want to die in it?"

He noticed that he was at a church.

"St. Cecilia's," he observed.

"It's Catholic. They believe in heaven."

"I was once madly in love with a girl named Cecilia. I wanted to be with her more than I wanted to be alone."

"Have I ever been here?" asked his father.

"It's a church. When was the last time you were in any church?"

"Aw, shaddup."

"I do believe, though I don't act on it, that it's a good idea to attend church regularly."

"And why's that?" I asked him.

"Because no one is ever sentenced to death for first-degree murder. You're sentenced to death because you never went to church. Or you were never seen helping a person in a wheelchair get over the curb. Or you didn't show enough emotion when terrible things were discussed. Or you had too many tattoos and a prison record. Or you weren't nice to your parents and you pissed off your teachers."

We fell in line with the others.

"As a child," Vincent whispered to me, "I had some small exposure to matters of faith. The old man might have been a godless communist in those days, but my mother took me to Lutheran services. Nothing happened. In fact, I was uneasy to see a crowd of people sitting and rising and sitting again in somber, orderly, if not grim, fashion, in perfect agreement to an unsolvable mystery, absolutely sure there was a hell for evil people and a heaven for those who believed in a particular tale, or at least said they believed. The mystery isn't death, Quinn; the miracle isn't birth. The miracle and the mystery are one. Life. And the answer is here, not hereafter."

"Okay, and here we are," I said.

Mourners were backed up to a standstill in the vestibule where everyone stopped to sign the book. Vincent moved in front of his dad. "I'll sign for you, too, okay?"

"No, it's not okay. I can sign for myself. I still know how to write my own goddamn name."

The old man was studying his son's signature. "You write terrible. Look, you don't dot the i, you can't even read what it says, it just looks like a squiggly line. What are you, a doctor?"

"Just sign it, all right? People are waiting."

"They can wait, don't rush me. Penmanship counts. What kind of a stupid pen is this? Is this supposed to be fancy?"

"Dad . . ."

"I don't know how they expect a person to write with this goddamn thing."

"Sign it!"

"For my money, a number two pencil, sharpened with a Buck knife, that's still the only way to go."

"Sign it, Dad, goddammit, sign it, will you?"

I scanned the names when I signed it, the way everybody does. Nothing popped out at me. We went into the church proper and passed by the open casket. She was pretty but had no lines of character on her face, American cute bled of all perkiness, youth not gone but halted. I turned my head and looked at Vincent as he looked down into the casket. He seemed pained, remembering, I'm sure, his own chance meeting with her when she was all she should be.

Sitting next to him in a pew, I could see Vincent already regretting that he had come.

He was perspiring, though it was not at all warm in the church. Looking into the casket of a murder victim should not have been a crisis to his basic conviction, a simple belief that executions only added to the general store of pain and misery in the world. But what Vincent did for a living, with my help, was always difficult. He used to argue that prosecutors ought to be required to witness the executions of those successes they'd worked so hard to achieve. It was a useless argument, something you just threw into the endless debate on the subject. It was no more likely to change a prosecutor's methods or goals than Vincent's attending the funerals of victims would change his own. Still, he was sweating in a chilly island church.

5

Arnie Stimick was red-eyed and choking back tears as he eulogized Eileen. She was innocent, he said, hardworking, a friend to all, a girl eager for life, a girl who decided to work for a year before attending college or design school, to earn some money, to be on her own for a while, a girl with no enemies, a trusting girl. Most of it I had already heard, when I'd dropped into his office and caught him before he could blow his brains out.

The church was full to overflowing. All her high school friends sat in clusters, holding on to each other for support. Family, friends, so many islanders who'd known her all her life, the Pioneer Building group. And a Channel Five news crew.

For a moment even Clinton seemed to have broken through his detachment, that emptiness of body and spirit sabotaged like an inside job from a betrayal of brain chemistry. But when Vincent whispered, "How're you doing, Dad?" he answered aloud, "At night, a lady comes into my room." I heard a few titters behind me, nervous reactions. Da frick, I have them, too.

After the service, we each took one of Clinton's elbows and tried to steer him through the exiting crowd. In one of those odd moments of social centrifugal force, the cluster of people surrounding the girl's mother and father fell away and we were exposed, so to speak.

We let go of the old man, setting him adrift in the shifting tide of mourners. I said hello to Abby and introduced Vincent as a friend.

"We all worked in the same building downtown," he said.

"This is Eileen's father, Sam Jones," she said.

We shook hands all around. Anyone would know, by the way she included his last name, that they were divorced, thrown together publicly too soon after the breakup, and without the benefit of a happy occasion like a graduation or a wedding. Sam Jones maybe said, Thanks for coming, I don't know, can't remember, but he quickly moved away and into another cluster of people.

Scandinavians abound around here, as everybody knows. That blond hair, that fine-featured and stoic face, that centered quality of body. For a man of a certain age, let's say Vincent's, she wasn't hard to look at.

"You're divorced, aren't you?" Vincent asked. Da frick. He'd been showing signs of inappropriate behavior, and I cut him a lot of slack, knowing the pressures of his job, but come on.

"Yes," she answered, forthrightly.

"God, I'm sorry. I mean, I'm sorry about everything, but . . . I don't know why I said that."

You see, he wasn't entirely clueless.

"I guess it shows, even to a stranger. It's only been a year."

"Sometimes it shows forever."

Vincent really had no talent for small talk, which is probably why I liked him a little. Everything he talked about was a matter of life and death.

Abby said, "Thank you for coming." She shook our hands again and moved away.

"You slay me with your lack of social skills," I told him. "You are too weird for words."

"Most of what comes out of my mouth is absurd. I can't help it."

"Go figure, since your profession is all

about finding the right sentence."

"I'm such a fool."

"Leave her alone, why don't you?"

"What? Of course I'll leave her alone. I'll never see her again."

"If only."

"Why would I?"

"Because you just fell in love with her, you asshole."

"I did not. Why would you say such a thing?"

"The damaged are drawn to each other, and everybody can see it."

"Me? Damaged? You assume too much."

"Assume this. You already want to see her again. You're wondering how that could happen."

"And you call yourself a detective?"

"Yeah, and I got you dead to rights."

In our little logroll we'd forgotten about his father, who was now kind of lost. That plastic bracelet he wore would do him no good out here in the world. We fought a small panic until we found him wandering about the back of the church grounds, perfectly at ease, nodding hello to strangers, without a clue as to where he was or why. For a moment he seemed enviable, to both of us.

"You want me to ride back with you?" I asked.

"No."

He was a little mad at me, I guess. We went around to the front again and I was about to go find the bus when we noticed a stir going through the crowd, and Stimick, cell phone to his ear, was leaving a big wake behind him as he pushed through the crowd and sought out Abby. He put a protective arm around her shoulders and steered her away from all the others.

"What's up?" I asked Bernard.

"They got the dude!"

6

Our group gathered in the forward seating area of the ferry. It wasn't long before Vincent came up from the car deck to join us. He'd left the old man asleep in the car. I made room for him between Bernard and me. Arnie Stimick stood before us, numb with grief, shaking with anger. The skyline of Seattle was behind him, shrouded in mist. He struggled for words.

"A scumbag," he said, "your basic scumbag."

He ran his hand over his glistening scalp.

I was relieved they'd arrested somebody, and so quickly, but, excuse me, I was bummed that they'd done it with absolutely no help from me.

"His name is Merck," said Arnie. "Randy Merck. Long, long police record. He's been assaulting girls since he was thirteen. *Thirteen,* he started. Nobody saw this coming? He was out on *parole* for attacking another girl, after spending thirty-four months in prison. *Thirty-four months . . .* you get that for, what, writing bad checks?"

We floated on a sea of sadness, the current against us, and before we could fight the sadness we had to first let it take us where it would. I gave a sideways glance to Vincent. He drifted with us, but on a different vessel. He knew that sooner or later, in a matter of days, he would get the call from some public defender: save Randy Merck's life. The message might already be on his machine.

"How did they get him?" I asked.

"Purely by accident. He still had her car and was in a Bellingham mall parking lot trying to siphon gas out of an RV. Security and the RV owner held him for police."

Vincent said, "What about Abby? Should she be left alone on the island?"

"One of my girls is staying with her tonight."

Vincent seemed relieved, at least about that.

"This animal comes upon Eileen, a girl who's just put in an honest day's work and is looking forward to her evening. A crowded neighborhood. A well-lit street. What the hell is wrong with this city? Why are we allowing this to happen?"

We sat benumbed, in grief and silence, except for some supporting mumbles of anger and incredulity.

"I don't know about the rest of you, but I'm not going to take this. That scumbag puke set upon the wrong girl. That girl has friends. I'm not going to weep for Eileen then let it happen to some other poor girl. I'm not going to stand by and watch her killer get away with murder."

"What makes you think he'll get away with it?" asked Vincent. I wished he'd shut up.

"Watch, he'll become the victim. Me, and you, and you . . ." He looked stonily into the eyes of each of us. I was kind of fascinated by his rage. "We will all become the cause of this, and he'll become the victim. Even Eileen, they'll blame it on her. They'll say she brought it on herself. They'll say anything, use all our own resources, spare nothing to deny it ever happened, and if it did happen it was some kind of unavoidable accident. Well, I'm here to serve notice. That son of a bitch will hang if I have to do it myself!"

Vincent sank down into himself. The hangman's advocate always did that to him.

"I am going to be at this trial," Stimick went on, "every single day of it. I want those jurors to know that Eileen had friends, and her friends are not going to forget her."

We all nodded and some muttered that they, too, would take time to attend the trial.

"What we should do," said Stimick, "is we should organize our attendance. We should check with one another and make sure that every hour during the trial some of Eileen's friends are there in the courtroom, staring down the jury. We'll make it a court watch."

"Will that do any good?" someone asked.

"If this whole system is a game of manipulating jurors and judges and the press, then friends of the victims have to get into the game. We have to pressure-play them, full-court press, because every time one of these pukes wins, any number of women get hurt or killed."

I thought about it for a moment and I had to agree with him. The court system *is* a game. Everything in American life has taken the game as its central metaphor. War is a game. The stock market is a game. Politics certainly is a game. Romance is a game — a man gets to first base, then tries to score. Everything is a game but games themselves. Games are serious business. Football, baseball, basketball, the players and the coaches never miss an opportunity in interviews to point out, "It's a business."

"Maybe he'll plead guilty and there won't

be a trial," said Vincent. It may have been wishful thinking. Anyway, he seemed incapable of shutting up.

"I hope you're right. We'll see."

People went for more coffee, some clam chowder. I waited until Arnie was alone, sitting and watching the Seattle skyline grow larger.

"Arnie."

"Yeah, Quinn."

"I'm really sorry."

He nodded.

"I didn't do much, I'm afraid."

"You did what you could. Thanks. The important thing is, they got him."

"Yeah."

"Now all we have to do is make sure he hangs."

"Can't help you on that," I said.

"Sure you can. Just show up."

By the end of the passage, we were drained. We all trudged off the ferry together, down the long incline, and then along the waterfront before turning up Yesler toward our building. We naturally fell into groups of twos and threes. Vincent, Bernard, and I fell into step together, lagging behind the others.

"Well . . . this is going to be interesting," I said.

"I didn't say boo, man, I'm stayin' out of this," said Bernard.

Apart from him and me, no one there had a clear idea of who Vincent was and what he did for a living.

"Everyone's angry," said Vincent. "It's normal."

"I'd lie low if I were you," I said. "Just in case."

"I always do."

"Fuckin' Arnie, he finds out you a coddler . . . ," said Bernard.

"I don't coddle criminals. That's not even half true."

"He don't know that."

"I want them punished. I want society protected, just like everybody else."

"Old Arnie, though . . ."

"Look, I don't want murderers going free. I want them standing in the corner. Forever. If a bit of sun falls on the murderer's face, through a sliver of a window, that would be all right. Let him enjoy it. If not, that would be all right, too."

We weren't going to argue; we just moved along at our slow pace. A seagull landed on the railing, looked at us as a food source. No luck. We walked on. The seagull stayed.

"I got two good seats for Sunday's game,"

145

Bernard said. "The Lakers. How hot is that, man?"

Vincent said, "No, I don't go to games anymore."

"I could care less," I said.

"Huh? Five minutes on the bus, you're there."

"The season goes on forever, and every week they've got new players," Vincent said. "I can't keep track of them. Last time I went, they looked like just another bunch of working stiffs."

"He's right," I said. "They remind me of miners going down to the coal hole. They were, like, wishing the job was over. There was no joy in what they're doing."

"It's a business," Bernard said, in defense of the thing. "What'll you do with your Sunday, you don't go to the game?"

"Drink coffee, read the newspaper, wait till Monday," said Vincent.

I chuckled, but I knew it was true. For me, too, pretty much. Clean my apartment, listen to the replay of *Prairie Home Companion,* take naps, cold showers, and more naps.

We crossed the street from Alaskan Way to under the viaduct. Arnie Stimick was way ahead of us, walking alone, a man on a mission.

"Fuckin' Arnie," said Bernard, "dude's

heart is broke."

"Arnie's got some problems," I said. "Generally."

"He was bonin' her."

Vincent looked offended.

"You sure, or just talking?" I asked him.

"He only hires sweet young things, acts like their daddy, you figure it out."

"He may just be a fatherly type," said Vincent.

"Yo, come to fathers," said Bernard, "where's yours at?"

"God! I left him in my car, on the ferry!"

He turned around and ran. We watched him and, of course, we laughed. He didn't run often, it looked like.

I'm sitting here trying to avoid saying it was the lull before the storm, but what the hell else was it? A storm was definitely coming, but for now I had nothing to do, except tag along with Vincent and check my answering machine.

I went with him to the courthouse, each of us carrying a latte. When we started from his office, I'd tried to give him three little words to remember, but he held up his hand. He wasn't in the mood. The day before he had seen his doctor and expressed his concerns about falling into Alzheimer's and losing his mind.

"So what did he tell you?"

"That I've gained some weight . . ."

"You look okay."

"He asked me about stress."

"Show me the job that doesn't come with stress."

"He thinks it preoccupies me, with murder

and all, that I can't turn it off, that I carry it twenty-four seven. I hate that expression."

"Yeah, but you do."

"Not every hour of every day."

"Every waking hour."

"It is kind of important, you know, like, life or death. I am alive, let everyone live, that's my credo."

"And if you were dead?"

"Fuck 'em all."

You had to laugh.

"He wanted to know how I was sleeping."

"I could have told him that."

"Have I ever slept with you?"

"You'd remember."

"I told him what really bothered me was the forgetting. Like leaving my father behind on the ferry. Jesus, the poor old guy was trembling when I found him. The ferry workers had to push the car off the boat and off to a corner of the landing, with Dad trying to steer, something he hasn't done in years, and never very well. Oh, they assured me it's happened before, more often than the crew appreciates. A commuter who's used to walking aboard takes his car one day and half an hour later he walks off and goes to work, forgetting he brought his car."

"See, *that's* the man with the problem, not you. How did your dad handle it?"

"He forgot about the whole thing two minutes later. One of the great benefits of the disease is you forget the scary things just as quickly as the good stuff."

"Small consolation."

"You said it. I told the doc, I go into a room for something, forget what, I stand there, turning in circles. I open my drawer for a file, forget which one. If I don't keep my checkbook between my teeth, I'll lose it. Sometimes I catch myself staring off into space, just like my old dad, not a thought in my head, nothing but fog. And sometimes this thing happens. I'll see somebody on the street, somebody I know, an acquaintance. He, or she, is just ahead of me, say, and doesn't see me. Do I call out, Hey, hi, how're you doing? Do I exchange pleasantries, stop for a cup of coffee, get caught up on things?"

"Do you?"

"I do not. I duck away like a fugitive. When I do talk to people, I can't make eye contact."

"You're making eye contact with me."

"I am? Then I'm cured."

"So relax, why don't you."

"He asked me if I ever thought about suicide."

You can only say one thing to that and I

chose not to.

"I told him I think a lot about suicide, not mine, but other people's."

"Other people's? Whose?"

"There's this houseboat on Lake Union, very close to the bridge, and for some reason desperate characters seem to want to aim for the roof of that particular little houseboat rather than land in the water."

Damn, it wasn't funny but you had to laugh. Again. I mean, picture it, like there was a bull's-eye on the roof.

"I often think about those people jumping, and I also think about the people who live inside the houseboat, having dinner there, and suddenly — *whump!* — another one lands on them, rocks the houseboat. 'Shit, call nine-one-one, tell 'em we have a ladder.' "

We stopped for a moment at the entrance to the courthouse.

"He asked me about drinking. I told him I forgot where the liquor was. He asked about my eating habits, about sex, my joint pains, morbid thoughts, religion . . . Hell, I was having déjà vu, like I was interviewing a client, but the client was me. At the end of it he wanted to put me on antidepressants."

"Good."

"I declined."

"Why?"

"What's the point? I'd only forget to take them."

8

The benches in King County courtrooms are angled forward, cutting in just below the shoulders. They were designed to take away the entertainment value of sitting in court. I only half listened to the woman testifying on her brother's behalf. Vincent paid closer attention. After all, he had coached her.

Martin Scarlotti, the accused, in the autumn of his life, was a nice enough man, and respected in the community. He had never before been in trouble with the law. He was now, big-time. He had "savagely" murdered two people, to use the DA's description. You ever hear of a civilized, graceful murder? He offed his girlfriend and the man with whom he suspected she was having an affair, and, yes, he had planned it with some precision. Finally, though, it was a crime of passion, and was to have included his own death, an element he'd botched.

Cutting your own throat takes no more than the pressure you need to cut somebody else's throat, but your arm just can't bring itself to full strength. No jury, in Vincent's opinion, was going to finish the job for him, and I had to go along with him on this one.

A lot of what the sister was testifying to, in order to build a case of a respectable man gone loony, would be reiterated when Vincent took the stand, as mitigating factors should the jury find him guilty: his exemplary army record, the pressure of paying two alimonies, his failure at romance with a much younger woman. This was an easy one. You could phone it in.

When the judge called a fifteen-minute recess, we followed the bailiff and the cuffed Scarlotti to an anteroom. He still wasn't quite sure what role we played in the process. Like most defendants, he accepted us as part of the defense team, underlings to the attorney. Only after being found guilty would it become apparent to him that Vincent was the key to his survival.

"How're you doing, Martin?" Vincent asked him, transparently cheerful.

Martin shrugged. He was a big man, larger than Vincent, bespectacled, balding, a second chin of prominence. Reminded me a little of Arnie Stimick. It was almost comical to picture this man storming into the new boyfriend's home after the love of his life, a perfectly plain woman whose illusion of beauty in Martin's eyes had to come from the seventeen-year difference in their ages, nearly the same difference as between Connors and that bitch he left me for. Martin had crashed their tryst wearing two chef knives strapped to his legs, like an absurd hyperactive middle-aged urban Rambo. Now, sitting one room away from the twelve who would determine his fate, he looked like a sad and ruined insurance executive, which indeed he was, ever since he windmilled those knives at the man and the woman who broke his heart.

"Martin, tell me something. Quinn here found that in elementary school and right through high school, you were known as someone pretty quick with his fists. True?"

He seemed confused. "That's ancient history. Back then, kids fought with their fists."

"Well, that's what I wanted to ask you about. Can you remember your last fistfight? Or your last, you know, act of violence, before all this happened?"

"Violence? I was in love! Doesn't anybody understand that? I was out of my head. I can't believe I did something like that."

During the testimony, Martin was embarrassed by the lengthy descriptions of the murder scene; he was ashamed when the prosecution displayed pictures showing a trail of blood that ended at a note the victim had written in her dying moments, in Crayola, to her children, who were spending the night with her ex-husband. Martin wept.

"I think they'll understand that, Martin."

"When I saw them together, something just snapped. I grabbed a knife in each hand. I swung wildly. It just happened."

Da frick. The shit-happens defense.

"Yes, I understand that. But tell me, what were your school days like? Did your mother make you lunch?"

Martin looked at him blankly. Lunch? Wasn't he listening?

Vincent hated it when all they wanted to talk about was the crime. I could see him squirming. Those were the details he most wanted to avoid. But it's inevitable, there's no stopping them.

"I swung wildly. I must have hit the whatchacallit artery in her neck, because the blood . . . God, it spurted everywhere. It got into my eyes even. I was so out of control. Not so much at him, but her. I loved her so much. How could she do that to me?"

To him? They see themselves as victims. I

wanted to smack him upside the head.

"I understand how you must have felt," Vincent said calmly, "but it would really help us to know something about your earlier life, while you were still in school, for example."

"They said I stabbed him a hundred and eighty times. How can that be? It felt like only three, four."

"Yes, yes, I'm sure, but can you remember, let's say, your junior prom?"

We were called back to court before Vincent could add a single item of mitigation to Scarlotti's biography. It wouldn't help to tell the jury that Martin *thought* he'd stabbed the victim only three or four times. Still, no real cause for concern. Martin's past life would speak for itself. He went to church. He contributed to charities. He volunteered at the library, sorting books for the sale.

Back in the courtroom Vincent continued to work out of his briefcase, but I slipped away before the lunch recess. On the ground floor, walking toward the exit to Third Avenue, I heard a familiar voice, amplified by a loudspeaker. Arnie Stimick.

"The friends of Eileen are not going to let the system ignore her! Not while all its mighty safeguards rally to protect the rights of her killer, an animal who has repeatedly attacked defenseless women and who has been sent back again and again by the system to do it again and again. They'll say he's insane, but it's the system that's insane! Now we must rally, too. We who knew and loved Eileen must rally to stop the insanity of the system! Stop the insanity! Stop the insanity!"

A crowd of a hundred office workers had gathered during their lunch break. In a light drizzle under gray skies, they filled the sidewalks on both sides of the street.

I saw Bernard and some others I recognized from the building. I made my way through the crowd and came up behind them.

"¿Qué pasa?"

"Yo, Quinn," said Bernard. "A bona fide protest. Is this what the sixties were like?"

"I was a wee child in the sixties, you asshole. I don't remember nothin' but Barbies."

"You played with dolls?"

"Fuck you."

"Power to the people," he said, shooting up a fist in a generic sort of way, impossible to take seriously.

"We must take back this neighborhood and fight for a safe place to work and to live!" Arnie shouted out. You had to admire his passion, even though you wondered where it came from. "Public policies have created an environment where rapists and murderers can attack us in broad daylight. Do we run scared?" The crowd yelled back an enthusiastic *No!* "Or do we fight back?" Now, of course, they yelled back with even more vigor, *Fight back!* "Then call them, call the councilmen, call the mayor, call the police, call the county commissioner, call them and tell them that you're not going to tolerate the slaughter of your friends. Call them and tell them that you are a friend of Eileen and you are going to fight back!"

I looked over my shoulder and saw Vincent standing in front of the courthouse, watching the demonstration in dismay. He had just received the call he'd been dreading.

9

"Just now?" I asked.

We left the demonstration and were walking back toward the office.

"Not ten minutes ago. I was having trouble hearing her because I was walking toward the noise of the protest. But then I stopped and backed up against a wall and blocked out everything else."

"Wendy Maron."

"The same."

She was a public defender Vincent had worked with before, and I knew her slightly. I found her overbearing and full of herself, but Vincent had a history with her, a few victories and one hopeless defeat, a killer with no mitigating circumstances or redeeming qualities who was now waiting on Death Row and had recently gotten a new date, now that he was down to 290, which the state qualifies as an allowable weight. Any heavier than that runs the risk of decapitating the condemned, which might be seen as cruel and unusual punishment. The Fat Man, as everybody took to calling him, had taken on the state by means of a unique ploy: his canteen privileges. Over the years of waiting on Death Row, he had consumed massive amounts of Butterfingers and Kit Kat bars, pork rinds and corn chips. Dead man Bruce had larded on more than a hundred pounds and filed for a stay of execution, which he won. The experts argued long after hours over whether indeed his deranged head would come off with the snap of the noose.

The Fat Man's plan might have worked had he not destroyed his liver in the process. He demanded a new one, or rather a good used one, and that set off a whole new whirl of hearings, expert testimony, and a fair amount of controversy, ending in the finding that this particular individual was not a good candidate for a publicly donated liver. The ruling was appealed by the ACLU, which held fast to the idea that Bruce was as entitled as anyone else to a liver up for grabs. Appeal denied. Medical testimony, at that time, estimated his remaining life span at less than a year, and now, having taken away his canteen privileges, the state was in a hurry to execute him before he died. Da frick.

"Did you try to refuse?" I asked him.

"Not really. I didn't feel I could."

"I could have refused."

"You still can."

"But PIs are a lot easier to find than MIs."

"Around here."

"What did she say, more or less?"

"Said I'd have a lot to work with, a real product of the penal system. He's been begging for help since he was first arrested."

"When was that?"

"Age thirteen, for rape. Thirteen. Just imagine. When I was thirteen I still didn't know you could do more with it than pee. That and hide it from the other guys in the showers."

"So you said count me in."

"No, I told her I had a problem."

"What kind of problem?"

"That's what she asked. I told her I kind of knew the victim. She wanted to know how well."

"Da frick, you only talked to her once, about smoking. At least that's what you told me."

"And that's what I told her, which happens to be the truth."

"But did you tell her you had a moment with the girl's mother?"

"I did not have a moment. I told her I was at the funeral, with my father, and I met the parents."

"Met them both but connected with her."

"So you say."

"And Wendy said what?"

"She couldn't understand why I would go to the funeral."

"Neither could I."

"Common decency. She worked in the building. Wendy asked me if, because of all that, Randy Merck was someone I wouldn't mind seeing executed."

"She doesn't know you very well."

"Neither do you, so don't presume."

"You told her you'd do it, I know that much."

"I'm the only one who does this up here. She'd have to go to Los Angeles for Casey Cohen if I turned her down, and she doesn't have the budget for that."

"So you said you'd do it."

"I asked her if she'd heard of the 'Friends of Eileen.' "

"Had she?"

"No one has, not yet. They will now, thanks to Arnie's taking it to the street. I explained that a grassroots movement was going through birth pangs. She dismissed it as just one more groundswell of righteous indignation that follows newspaper coverage of a lurid crime and soon fades away."

"Yeah, I kind of did that myself."

"I told her I was part of it, kind of. Everybody in the building was. I mean, who wanted to say he was *not* a friend. I would have liked to know her better, to really have been her friend. She seemed like such a sweet kid. She brightened the space around her."

"You told her all that?"

"Most of it. Hell, she said, she'd join up herself, if all they want is a safer city, as long as they're not calling for Randy's head on a stick."

"Sure they are."

"That's what I told her. They plan to be in court every session."

"She's okay with that?"

"She said I'll be open for criticism, I may lose a couple of friends, and this is not a popular thing we do."

"What friends?"

"You're not my only friend, you know."

"So when do we meet this scumbag?"

"Tomorrow."

10

Vincent once told me that most murderers, once captured, have about them a sweet and beautiful calm, a quiet acceptance of whatever the future holds, an openness and vulnerability common to the terminally ill.

Randy Merck was a lot like that. He could smoke or not, sit or stand, listen or whisper; "whatever" was fine with Randy Merck. He smiled shyly when Wendy introduced us as part of the team. His hand, when I shook it, was soft and yielding and cold as a corpse. He said he was grateful that everyone was going through so much trouble for him.

He was not, in my opinion, an unattractive man. A bit undersized, maybe, with darting feral eyes, but even so he struck me as a man who could have met women and wooed them, and won their affections in the time-honored way. We would eventually discover why he hadn't.

Wendy started the ball rolling with,

"Randy, why don't you tell us, as nearly as you can recall, exactly what happened that day?"

"Where do you want me to start?"

"Anywhere you want to."

He took a long slug from the bottle of Geyser water he was holding, swished it through his mouth for a moment, then started to tell his story.

He had every intention, he said, of going that morning to the shit job the state had arranged for him at Roy's Auto Body Repair, but on his way from the half-way house to the bus stop he started thinking about what a sweet deal old Roy had, hiring ex-cons and letting the taxpayers pay part of their salary. Roy acted like he was doing you this very large one, letting you spend eight hours a day in his shit shop, learning his chump trade, the only advantage to which was that it was honest, and even then only partway so. Sure, it was cool to be out of Walla Walla, but the job they gave him at Roy's was worse than solitary confinement. The assholes working there might as well be doing life without parole.

This is how he told it to us.

The more he thought about it, he said, as he waited for the bus, the more he believed he deserved a day off, to sort things out in his head. He'd tell Roy he was sick, no big deal. He walked away from the bus stop and went over to Muscatel Meadows, the park across the street from the county courthouse, but since he wasn't known there, nobody would front him anything. He walked over to the Public Market and passed through it, looking for a likely tourist vic, but everybody was with somebody, clutching their purses to their fat bodies, so he went on to Steinbrueck Park and habla-ed a little broken Spanish, but the Latinos didn't like him.

He had only a couple of bucks on him, which he blew on Rainier beer. The steel-gray Seattle light was fading fast to night and it began to rain again, that old deliberate drizzle like needles in the face, which kind of freaked him out. He'd spent so much time inside that he wasn't used to weather. In short, he was feeling blue. He wished he had a girlfriend, a nice girl with a steady job, someone he could talk things over with, reveal secrets to, borrow money from. That's when he ran into Mr. Voss.

At this point Vincent stopped him, having picked up something in his voice. I picked up the same thing. "Who's Mr. Voss?" Vincent asked him.

"Go ahead, Randy, tell Vincent about Mr.

Voss," Wendy said. She had heard the story before and she seemed amused that Vincent would stop him at that point.

"What about him?"

"Everything, just so they know about Mr. Voss."

Vincent looked at her for a clue, but she kept her eyes on the legal pad on which she was keeping notes.

"He's this older guy, helped me out of some jams. We hang together sometimes, even though he's old."

"How old?" Vincent asked.

"I don't know, fifty."

"How long have you known Mr. Voss?"

"God, forever, I've been knowing him since I was a kid in Bremerton."

"What's his first name?"

Now Wendy looked up from her pad. Randy examined his torn cuticles. "I don't know," he said. "Yeah, I know, it sounds bogus, but when you're a kid you respect your elders. I only ever called him Mr. Voss."

"Were you very close?"

"He was like a father to me," Randy said, flatly, as though there were better relationships to have.

"Where is he now?"

"Wish I knew, 'cause he could tell you I didn't kill that girl."

168

For a long moment we waited in silence. I expected Wendy to move her client along, but she didn't, which was unusual because most public defenders, like their private counterparts, always have one eye on the clock, though for different reasons. It fell to Vincent to refire the narrative.

"Look, Randy," Vincent said, leaning intimately toward him, "you might find this hard to believe, but neither Wendy, nor Quinn, nor I really care that you killed Eileen Jones. It doesn't matter to us. That's done and can't be undone. All that matters to us is that we save your life. We can do a better job of that if we know everything — the absolute truth."

"I'm telling you the truth. I'm no angel but I never killed nobody."

"All right. So you've skipped work, you're broke, you're blue, you're hanging around, you've had a few beers, and you run into Mr. Voss. Where was this?"

"Outside the 7-13 Bar, on Second Avenue."

"What was Mr. Voss wearing?"

"Same thing he's always wearing. A navy-blue raincoat . . . and one of those Frenchman hats."

"A beret?"

"Yeah, a beret, the kind a Frenchman

169

wears. A black one. And shades. Mr. Voss always wears shades, all the time. Don't ask me what color his eyes are, I don't know. And that beret. He always wears that, 'cause he's bald on top."

"So he doesn't always wear it."

"Huh?"

"You know he's bald on top."

"He wears it all the time, except sometimes."

"What did you and Mr. Voss talk about?"

"Nothing special. We had a couple more beers at the 7-13, on him, and then went for a walk to see what we could get into. We saw this girl and kind of followed her for about a block . . ."

"Why?"

"Dunno. We followed her till she went into a building, and then we followed this other girl in the other direction, till she met up with a dude in front of this restaurant, so then we wandered on up Pike to Capitol Hill, lookin' inside cars for something to rip off. We saw this car and like it had all the windows down, in the rain and everything, so we looked inside. I mean, there's a car in the rain with the windows all down, and guess what? The keys was in it. Not in the ignition but on the floor. Mr. Voss says, Let's go for a ride. So we got in the car and took off. He drove. I can drive but I'm out of practice and I don't have a license. We was headin' up Broadway and I looked in the backseat and found a purse back there, on the floor, and it had some cash in it and a credit card, so, shit, we just kept on rollin'. We used her money to score some weed and some Xanax. You know the difference between true love and Xanax?"

A joke? The asshole had a joke?

"No, Randy, what is the difference?" Vincent asked indulgently.

"Xanax is forever."

The perv enjoyed a snotty little giggle.

"Anyway, that week is kind of a blur."

"Whatever you remember."

"We drove around, no place to go. We were circling our way north. Mr. Voss had this idea we should boogie on up to Canada. The money ran out before we got there so we was breaking into vending machines and panhandling in the malls. You know, ran out of gas and could you help us get back to Wenatchee, that kind of shit, which was true 'cause we really were out of gas. That's how we got caught. How I got caught. As usual, Mr. V. got away. The fucker has a sixth sense. Either that or he set me up, which I would not put past him. If that's what he wanted, it's workin' pretty good."

"Where were you when this happened?"

"When what happened?"

"When you ran out of gas?"

"We was in Bellingham, at a mall there, and down to the fumes. Mr. Voss cops this length of hose and tells me to go siphon some gas for the car while he goes to boost us some road food. I'm parked next to a motor home so I got good cover and I'm suckin' away on the hose and got myself a refill goin'. Next thing I know this rent-a-cop and two bag boys from Safeway got me surrounded. I don't got a prayer. You think I could get a Coke?"

This story was told in utter boyish sincerity. None of us believed a word of it. I wished I had, like Wendy, the comfort of cigarettes, which she smoked one after the other, sharing them with Randy Merck.

After, the three of us had lattes together at a street cart. It was unusually mild, in the low fifties, with a thick gray mist hanging over the city.

"What do you think?" I asked her.

"That's our defense. He didn't have a thing to do with it. He's guilty of car theft, nothing more."

"You believe him?"

"I didn't say that."

"You want me to start working anyway?"

172

asked Vincent.

"Yeah, sure, start your work."

"Okay."

We sipped our lattes.

"I can go look for Mr. Voss," I said.

"Do it. It would be nice to know he exists."

"I'll start building the bio," Vincent said.

"Then we're in business."

"Was Eileen raped?" I asked.

"There was no sex, at least not as we know the practice."

"What was in her purse?" I asked.

"Her purse? I really don't know."

"There's going to be a lot of pressure for a death sentence," Vincent said.

"Pressure, schmessure."

11

I spent half a day on the computer and two days in Bremerton. I would have rather the reverse.

Randy, I found, was out of the school system and into the justice system by the age of thirteen, so in his hometown he was only vaguely remembered and only by a few and only as a sneaky little kid with a stink eye. No one remembered a Mr. Voss.

I found Randy's boyhood home, a modest clapboard place, but better than most of the houses in the mining town where I grew up. Da frick, it was nicer than our house on East Coal Street, two doors down from the spring-and-muffler shop. But I could sense it was nowhere near as happy. Of all the things I have in life, or ever had, the one I value most highly is my happy childhood. I knocked on some neighbors' doors, but one after another the current residents turned out to have moved there after Randy and his family were already gone. I'd gone through seven or eight before I got lucky. An old pensioned boatyard worker, rolling an oxygen tank behind him, opened the door and seemed pleased to have a visitor. I told him why I was there and he invited me in for a longneck Bud, which I was happy to accept.

He didn't know them all that well. He was several houses away so there was no talking over the back fence.

"I don't think anybody knew them that well, really, but we all knew about them."

"Oh? Why's that?"

"They had a busy social life, let's say, people coming and going all the time, but it never included the neighbors."

"Drugs?"

"Oh, no, nothing that ordinary."

"What, then?"

"Well, I'll tell you what." I waited for it. "They were devil worshippers."

"Say what?"

"You heard me right. They worshipped old Satan."

"How do you know that?"

"You could hear them, chanting and howling like wolves and groaning like bears. They were all animals in that house. They had sex orgies."

"They did?"

"Oh, yes, and worse. And then one day the wife was just gone. Just disappeared. I had the nerve to ask why we hadn't see her lately, and he just said mind your own business. I think he killed her, chopped her up, and the rest of 'em ate her. But that wasn't why he finally went to prison."

"The father? Randy's father went to prison?"

"Still there, as far as I know."

"Why did he go to prison?"

"Rape. Child rape."

"Don't tell me . . ."

"Oh, yeah. He raped Randy. Others too."

That was already kind of a lot to take, but he had one more thing to tell me: Randy's father was a cop.

We had another beer together, and then I went down to the BPD and explained that I had twenty-two years in as a foot cop and now was a snooper, but that sister cop stuff didn't cut much ice with them. They'd washed their hands of George V. Merck long ago. All they could tell me was that he now was incarcerated on McNeil Island.

I spent the night in a Super 8 and had dinner at a Domino's, all on the county.

I knew that eventually Vincent would have to interview the father anyway, so I stayed over and in the morning drove to Steila-coom and took the prison boat to the island, which is the only island prison left in North America. It started as a territorial prison back in the early nineteenth century. The first inmate there did twenty months for selling liquor to the Indians. It then became a federal prison, and for the last twenty-five years or so it's been part of the Washington State correctional system.

I laid out some credentials, told my story, and had no problem getting in to see Randy's dear old dad, who had been chilling the past fifteen years in the segregation unit, for his own protection, since he had at least two reasons for another inmate to bury an implement in his liver: he was a cop and he was a short eyes, queer for little boys.

We sat on opposite sides of a desk, with a guard nearby. Merck Senior had none of the pliability of his son; he was flinty and cruel. He sat with his powerful arms folded across his chest. He'd occasionally rub his gray mustache with the edge of his hand.

I asked him if he knew about his son. He smiled. He chuckled. Sure, he knew. He watched TV, he read the papers.

"You think it's funny?"

"Hysterical. I didn't think the little shit had it in him."

177

Ah, fatherly pride. I wanted to slap him upside the head, an impulse I suffer frequently and seldom satisfy. I'd planned to lay some groundwork for Vincent, but suddenly I just flat didn't want to be there anymore. I wanted to be back on the boat. Having a father like that was mitigation enough. I got right to the point.

"Randy's alibi is someone named Mr. Voss. Do you know who Mr. Voss is?"

"Mr. who?"

"Voss." I spelled it for him.

"Doesn't ring any bells with me, but I ain't seen Randy in a long while."

"I have the feeling Mr. Voss goes back pretty far. Randy says he's known him since he was a kid. He was an older man, like your age, maybe older."

"Oh . . ."

"Yes?"

"People don't always use their right names. I might of known him by a different name."

"What people?"

"There were a lot of them."

"A lot of what?" Exasperation was coming out of my ears.

The son of a bitch smiled again. "You know, older men who like boys."

"Pedophiles?"

"That's what they call them."

"And you ought to know."

"Not anymore, I'm on ice. But I had my fun."

He made my skin crawl.

"What do you mean, there were a lot of them?" I asked.

"A lot of them. Randy was a cute kid."

"You gave him to pedophiles?"

"I didn't *give* him to nobody. I don't *give* away nothin'."

12

I stood by the rail of the boat, on the lee side, in case I had to puke. I was also having a killer hot flash. I thought about throwing myself overboard and starting all over again.

Rather than board another ferry in Bremerton, I drove back by way of Tacoma and parked the PT in the underground parking at the apartment. I knew Vincent would still be in his office, so I trotted up the ramp, walked the length of the alley, one hand on my LadySmith, and crossed the street. I took the elevator up to his floor.

He was behind his desk. Spread across it were pictures of the crime scene. I got the upside-down view. There wasn't any way to look at them that eased the effect.

Her raincoat and skirt were bunched up around her thighs. Her head was twisted in an unnatural position. She was splattered with mud.

Vincent looked like he was trying to comprehend so much evil, one human being to another, stranger to stranger. Evil? Meet the father.

"Milk . . . screen . . . tree," I said. Toss any anchor.

"How'd it go?" he asked.

"You first."

"The DA's not waiting to mull it over. He's going for the death penalty."

"What, and you're surprised?"

"No. I knew he would. He didn't have to think any longer, he said, because if anybody ever deserved the death penalty, surely it was Randy Merck. All prosecutors say that, though. *If anyone ever deserved the death penalty . . .* It might be something they learn in law school."

"Sometimes they have a point."

"I always wonder, though, why this one and not the other one? Why not Steven Spellman, for example?"

Spellman was another one of Vincent's clients. He had killed three women, posing them dead in sexual partnership with the weapons of their own destruction.

"Why was Spellman off the hook? Not because of anything I did. It was simple economics."

The DA, in exchange for Spellman agree-

181

ing to let all three cases be tried simultaneously rather than to go through the time and expense of separate trials, dropped his demand for the death penalty. Played the game that way. Won, you could say.

"And Spellman's victims, let's face it, were all prostitutes. They didn't have so many devoted friends as Eileen, and none quite so unrelenting as Arnie Stimick."

"Everything is iffy, ain't?"

"So . . . where is our Mr. Voss?"

"Dunno. But it's possible he does exist."

"Nobody remembers him?"

"It was hard enough to find anybody who remembered Randy Merck."

Vincent nodded. It was not uncommon, especially with unmotivated killers, to go through life unnoticed.

"But nobody, nobody, remembers any Mr. Voss, or even anybody else buddying up with Randy."

"I have a theory about Mr. Voss."

"So do I, but go ahead."

"In the dark night of the soul, where it's always three o'clock in the morning, according to F. S. Fitzgerald and backed up by my own experience, everybody calls out for somebody . . . Mommy, Daddy, Christ, God, Holy Blessed Virgin Mother, Teddy the Bear . . . but I don't think Randy had emotional access to any of those helpers, and so he called out for Mr. Voss. Mr. Voss, who might be a figment of his imagination, a protector conjured up by a frightened little boy. Mr. Voss, who might have been real at one time, a teacher, a neighbor, a shop-keeper . . . anyone . . . a grown-up, a big man who could protect Randy, tell him what to do. In short, a proper father. He's been calling on Mr. Voss since he was four or five." He put his head back and howled plaintively, "Mr. Voss-s-s-s! Make it stop!"

"I like it. He could be a composite of them all, or just one of them, to whom he some-how became attached."

"Them who?"

"The pedophiles his father rented him out to."

Heavy sigh. Slight sickness in the stomach, which passes.

"Where'd you get this?"

"Horse's mouth. The fucking father."

"Quinn."

"Sorry. It's upsetting."

"I wish I could say this is the first time I ever heard of such a thing."

"Extra upsetting, personally, 'cause the father was a cop."

"Really?"

"We used to laugh at Spooky . . ."

183

"Spooky?"

"Spooky the Cop, back in Shenandoah. Big, illiterate Polack, hell knows how he got the job. Would rather backhand you than bring you in. But he was a decent man. A wise man. He kept a lot of us out of reform school, or worse. He cared, which is finally what a cop ought to do."

"And where is this other cop, Randy's father?"

"McNeil Island. May he croak there."

"For?"

"Child molestation. Including his own son."

Vincent closed the folder over the pictures of the crime scene, took a deep breath.

"You want to get some dinner? Maybe the trattoria?"

"I'm not hungry," I said. "Let's go up to the Alibi Room and get drunk."

"Okay. *Milk . . . screen . . . tree.*"

I managed to smile. Right on the money. I held my hand up for a high five. He gave it a gentle slap. That was as physical as we ever got with each other. Until that night.

13

Some people live for the telephone. I'm not one of them. When I was a kid, our one phone in the house was a wooden box attached to the wall. It had a crank that had to be exercised before a call could be placed. This was when we moved to the valley, over the hill to Ringtown. As a child I was instructed in its proper use and then ordered never to touch it except for emergencies. What is an emergency? Blood, and not just a little. Engulfing flame is another. Serious falls. The unexpected appearance of Uncle Eddie. When either my mother or father used the phone, on the rare occasions they did, they shouted into it and held one hand over the exposed ear.

This wooden contraption was soon replaced by a modern phone, a big black thing with a rotary dial. It was a party line, which we shared with three other families. Our ring was two shorts, I still remember. Any other ring we were not allowed to answer. More often than not, when you did pick up the phone to make a call, you heard one of the neighbors gabbing. If you had an emergency, along the lines I just described, you would ask them to hang up for a few minutes, which they would, though no one could resist picking it up again to hear what kind of emergency.

There were no extensions, just that one big black phone sitting on a small table with a single chair next to it, at the foot of the stairs. If the phone rang after nine pm it meant only one thing: someone, somewhere, had died. Long-distance calls were made only when life-changing information had to be transmitted immediately. When I traveled, I would call home person-to-person, collect, and ask for myself. My mother would tell the operator, of course, that I wasn't there. It was our cost-free method of letting everyone know I had reached my destination safely. When two-way communication was absolutely necessary, you timed it, talked fast, and finished within three minutes.

To this day I'm uncomfortable and rushed while on the telephone. I see it as something intruding and controlling and metered. I still jump when it rings. I find it impossible to allow a telephone to ring on. I will put myself in danger, in fact, to run to a ringing telephone. Once answered, I won't tarry to complete the call. I use the telephone often, in my work, but I don't like it and never will. I carry a cell phone like a curse of modern times.

I especially hate being awakened by a telephone ring. Sleep is hard enough to come by. So my answer when that happens is gruff. Sue me. I should care.

"I'm sorry," said Vincent on the other end.

"What for?"

"Sound of your voice tells me I ought to be sorry for something."

"It's not you, it's me."

"Uh-oh. That makes it worse."

For the past couple of months we'd been parrying these little romantic innuendos, ever since that night after the Alibi Room when, drunk as promised, we fell down to my kitchen floor with a tub of I Can't Believe It's Not Butter, and made what passes for middle-aged love between two friends and colleagues who'd had far too many strawberry Doc Greenies, which is what I start calling them after the third, with slurred instructions, embarrassed self-observations on hardness and/or wetness, questions and excuses on performances, till you begin to wonder, why the hell bother? I won't say I didn't feel anything, I just didn't feel enough. The night would not have a morning after. He had to know it was a one-off, and so he made the most of it, and I was a good sport: from sea to pasture, from crab to mare, then crawling to the living room where he could watch in the mirrored wall as we did the wheelbarrow. I didn't even look. Those days are long gone. After, exhausted and not a bit less drunk, we lay on the floor, him facedown. I petted his back and neck, rough with scar tissue. Earlier, when we'd kissed, I could feel it on his face, beneath the beard. I knew there was a story there.

"Vincent?"

"Hmmm?"

"Where'd you get all that scar tissue?"

A native northwesterner wouldn't have asked. I'm glad I did. I was having a touch of slut's remorse, and then he told me the story. Afterward, I was glad I'd let him fuck me. Big deal. He needed mercy that night, and release, and I needed the human touch. Let's be honest, *his* human touch. I needed intimacy as good as I could get and comfort as much as I could give.

"The fire" was how he answered my question at first. What fire, I wanted to know.

Halloween, in a children's haunted house, set up in a neighborhood center, a maze of plywood and cardboard passages, a labyrinth of spooky sounds and strobe lights, and Vincent and his little boy Johnny in his Batman costume, slowly making their way through it, Johnny building his courage until he was able to let go of his father's hand. Dark twisting corridors, laughing witches, hanging men, great spiderwebs. Vincent cautioned the boy to stay close; in the dark he could barely see him. On the walls they had stapled gooey plastic sheeting for the creepy tactile sensation. The floor was straw; hanging overhead, crepe paper.

Almost to the instant of Vincent having the thought — that this place was a firetrap — some parent just ahead of them lit a match. Vincent yelled to kill the light, but the match had already ignited some of the shredded hanging paper, which fell to the floor and ignited the straw and the plastic sheeting on the walls. Everything went up in flames. Pushing, falling, piling up in both directions, thick noxious smoke, children screaming, Vincent screaming for his son, frantically grasping to get his hand back. When he did, at last, he yanked the little boy into his arms in a bear hug. They could move neither forward nor back. Bodies were piling up, blocking them. Vincent rammed his shoulder against the plywood wall. He held his breath and tried to break through. On the third time the wall splintered and broke and they fell out, Vincent clutching Johnny to his chest, dragging him away as those outside beat the flames with raincoats. He struggled on all fours to regain his breath, spitting, gasping, eyes tearing. He heard the little boy cough. He was relieved. If he was coughing, he was alive. Then, able to open his eyes and focus, he saw that the little boy he'd saved was not his own.

I continued petting his neck and back. Words were no good for this. Nothing was.

I knew then why he had taken up his odd line of work. It was a penance.

Neither one of us could actually sleep with the other, or anyone else for that matter, and before dawn he padded down the hall to his own apartment.

"Why are you calling, Vincent?"

"They're selecting the jury today. I'll be talking to Randy. You want to come with?"

"I'll have to check my calendar."

"Yeah, right. See you there."

Phone etiquette says the one initiating the call has to terminate the call, but he didn't. He just held the line open.

"Vincent? You still there?"

"I also have a kind of job for you."

"Okay."

"Not really in your line, but . . ."

"Go on."

"I'm passing the buck on this one."

"I'm gonna need more details."

"I'll fill you in when I see you."

Which he eventually did. Not the sort of thing I'd imagined when I'd opened up shop.

14

I met Vincent in the lobby of the King County Courthouse.

The elevator door opened and we went up to the eighth floor. A second level of security had to be passed up there. The guard at the door ran his metal detector along my body and looked into my purse. He did a double take when he found my LadySmith. I showed him my permit and PI license, and since he knew Vincent, he let it slide. He went through the motions of checking Vincent, too. His right pocket set it off. He took out his keys and dangled them aloft. We were allowed inside.

Abby was sitting in the center of the first row, next to Arnie Stimick. A reporter sat behind them, looking bored with his assignment. When the courtroom door opened, everybody turned to look at us. Vincent's eyes went straight to Abby's. Was I the only one who saw what passed between them?

Well, I guess.

She turned her attention back to the proceedings. Arnie acknowledged us with a nod and silently invited us to sit beside him, but I made an ambiguous gesture to the rear and we sat there instead. Neither Wendy nor Randy noticed us, so for the moment we were just two more Friends of Eileen on court watch.

I noticed again how much Abby looked like her daughter, more like sisters than mother and daughter. She dressed well, though not expensively. She had a sense of style without crying for attention. She held herself erect and poised on the uncomfortable bench, taking in each juror as he answered questions from Wendy and the prosecutor. She never looked at Randy Merck, even with his back just a few feet in front of her.

The questions posed to the prospective jurors were routine and boring. We really had no professional reason for being there. The selection of the jury was of no particular interest to Vincent. He would take what he was given. We were there, I believed, just for him to see Abby again. Why did he drag me along? Was I auditioning for the role of beard?

Which reminded me. I whispered, "What

about that job you said you had for me?"

"Later."

I was wasting my time, sure, but I had nowhere else to go and nothing else to do, so I sat with Vincent fighting sleep while the attorneys droned on. Our mistake was in not slipping out of the courtroom before the lunch recess. I watched him watching her. He was lost in his own attraction to her. When it was already too late, we had to do a quick slide down the bench toward the wall. All arose and Randy Merck was led away. I sweated that we would wind up smiling and nodding to the accused like old friends. As it happened, Randy stood and faced the bench while he was cuffed, and when he was led out of the courtroom he kept his eyes dead on the floor ahead of him. A good thing, too, because how would we explain to Abby, not to mention Arnie, how we came to have a nodding acquaintance with the scumbag.

We ducked out right after Randy and his jailer, but Abby and Arnie caught up with us at the elevator.

"Thanks for coming," said Arnie.

"No problem," I said.

"Once it really begins, we're going to organize, have a chart and everything, and fill the courtroom with Friends. Have you met Abby Jones?"

"Yes . . . at the funeral," said Vincent. "Nice to see you again, Mrs. Jones."

"Abby, please."

"I'm sorry, have we met?" Arnie asked him.

"Vincent Ainge. I have an office in the building." He turned back to Abby. "I didn't really know your daughter," though he did and that was part of the mess. "I'm so sorry."

Vincent wandered blissfully for a moment in the calm of Abby's smile.

"What do you do?" she asked him.

"Pardon?" It was a question he often failed to hear.

"You said you have an office in Arnie's building."

"Yes . . . yes, I do . . . and I live just across the street, so my commute takes all of three minutes, on foot, of course, and that's counting a stop for a latte."

"How nice for you."

I knew then that she had to be native to the area, just like Vincent. Northwesterners have this maddening trait of withholding innocuous information for no apparent reason. The natives accept this trait in one another and live around it. In Los Angeles, where I lived for about ten years and where

I first became a cop, you know everything about a person in the first five minutes, including how good a lay he is, or at least how good a lay he thinks he is. Abby knew instinctively that Vincent had told her, for the moment, as much as he wanted her to know, and she would ask no more. Arnie, however, was from New York.

"But what kind of business are you in?"

I piped in and said, "We're both investigators."

"That must be interesting," she said.

"Has its moments," said I. We didn't get into it, thankfully, no questions about what kind of investigators we were.

"We're going over to the Metropolitan for lunch, would you care to join us?" Abby asked. I could see Arnie wasn't all that crazy about the idea.

Neither was I, even though the Met serves a fantastic club sandwich and my stomach was on a growl.

"Ah, problem is, we have an appointment," Vincent said.

He couldn't tell her with whom.

"Maybe, if it's not too long, you could meet us there, afterward."

Was she, in the midst of her bereavement, being pulled in Vincent's direction as well? Two people who should never have even

196

met? No good could come of it. I was tempted to choke it right then and there, to let her know why she really wouldn't want to have lunch with Vincent, or anything else.

"Sure, c'mon over," said Arnie, without enthusiasm.

Incredibly, Vincent said he would. I could have smacked him one. I let them know that for me it was impossible, without telling them why.

When the elevator doors opened and everyone piled inside, we held back. Arnie kept the door from shutting. "Getting on?"

"No, our appointment's upstairs."

Abby smiled again and the door shut. She did have a winning smile, I'll admit, but Vincent needed a stomp on the toes.

"Snap out of it, mister. What the hell are you thinking?"

"What?"

"You can't have lunch with her. You can't even talk to her."

"Why not?"

"Duh? You'd have to lie through your teeth."

"Just kind of delay the truth."

"Oh, so you will tell her, huh, you just don't know when."

"Eventually she'll know."

"Well, yes, everybody's going to know, like

when you take the stand and testify why her daughter's killer should go on living."

He pursed his lips.

"You're attracted to her, ain't?"

"I am."

"Da frick."

"Are you jealous?"

"Don't flatter yourself. That night . . . well, it came out of the blue . . . and it went right back where it came from. I'm talking about what's right and what's wrong. You and me, one time, considering the circumstances, there was nothing wrong with that, but this . . ."

"I don't think it's unethical for me . . ."

"Sure it is. It's wrong any way you look at it."

"Nothing's going to happen. Nothing ever happens. No woman can be with me, not for long. She would get sick of hearing about murder. My ex-wife did. And every woman after that."

"Who's the ex-wife?"

"Long story."

"All right, you want that woman, go for it. But quit this job. Right now."

"I can't. You know that."

"Then open your eyes, Mr. Magoo."

We went to the bridge and walked over to the jail.

15

Wendy was sitting with Randy. From a distance they looked more like a couple whose relationship was in crisis than a lawyer and client. They looked a lot like Connors and I must have looked near the end.

"We're a little down in the dumps," Randy explained in his quiet voice. He was fidgeting with his fingers, snapping his nails, twisting his thumb.

"Oh? They seemed like reasonable jurors to me," said Vincent.

"Wendy's disappointed in me."

"Not at all. Just doing my job," said Wendy. She nodded toward me and asked Vincent, "Is she going?"

"Going where?" said I.

"You didn't ask her?"

"Hey, Wendy, I'm right here."

"I'll talk to you later, Quinn," Vincent said. "I'm sorry. It's hard to find a good moment."

"All right," I said. Whatever it was, I knew it could wait until after this interview. It sounded like a shit errand, the sort of thing with which I have some experience.

"She don't think we can win," said the scumbag.

"Doesn't look all that promising, I'll admit, but hey, we're only in the first quarter," she said.

The game, again.

"Vincent? What do you think?"

"I don't know, Randy. I'm not a lawyer."

"You're not? What are you?"

Vincent didn't want to tell him yet. Wendy knew that.

"In cases like yours," she said, "Vincent and Quinn come on board, with a life ring."

"A life ring?"

"Like on a boat. If the boat sinks, Vincent has the life ring."

"Hmmmm . . . How's that work, Vincent?"

"We can talk about that later. What's the reason for all this pessimism?"

Wendy shook a cigarette out of her pack and offered it to Randy. She lit it for him. "I've got someplace I ought to be. You guys talk."

She had that sense common to public defenders and car salesmen of when to take a timely departure and let other forces hold sway.

After she left the room we sat in silence and watched Randy smoke, waiting.

"So no Mr. Voss, huh?" was what he finally said. "No alibi."

"You tell us," I said.

"You couldn't find him, huh?"

"No, but I found your father," I said.

"Yeah, he's a lot easier to find. How's he look?"

"Scary."

"Yeah. Everybody was scared of him. You have no idea, lady."

"Maybe some idea."

"Some people think he's the devil. For real."

"I could see the resemblance."

"What'd he say about me?"

"He said he didn't think you had it in you. Murder. He thinks you're a wuss."

Randy dropped his head. "I could have taken all the stuff, all the abuse, I could of sucked it up . . . if he just woulda . . . you know, cared for me a little, protected me."

I didn't even know yet what *all the stuff* was, but I did know it included sex with his father and his father's friends, for a price. Now, years later, this mess of a man says it would have been all right, if only . . . I've been called hard-hearted, but for the moment this one put the cuffs on me. Some scumbag.

"If Mr. Voss was going to help you this time," said Vincent, "he would have done it by now, Randy. Don't you think?"

"Mr. Voss . . ." Randy sighed out the name, a lament, a plea to unseen powers.

"Was there ever a real Mr. Voss?" I asked.

"Oh, yeah. Real as cancer." He took a long drag on his cigarette and said, "Is she married?"

"Who?"

"Wendy."

"Oh, I don't think she'd like me talking about her personal life with you," said Vincent.

"I don't think she is. She's kinda masculine. She hates my guts. She only puts up with me 'cause they pay her to. They pay her and she does her thing. Who pays you, Vincent?"

"They pay me, too, and I do my thing."

"But with you, it's different."

"In a positive way, I hope."

"Oh, yeah. You care . . . seem to."

"I do care, Randy. I don't want you to hang, no matter what you did."

"What about your personal life, you can't talk about hers?"

"My personal life? I don't have one. Not much of one anyhow, and a lot of it I seem to be forgetting. But if it will make you feel more comfortable, I'm happy to talk about what there is."

"I guess I'm just interested in people. You're gonna come see me off 'n on, huh?"

"Yes, we will spend a lot of time together."

"You'll want to know all about me."

"Yes, as much as I possibly can."

"See what makes old Randy tick, huh? You find out, tell me, okay?"

"There are reasons why you are who you are, why you did what you did."

"You think I killed that girl."

"I don't really care."

"Huh?"

"I don't care. I've tried to explain that to you. Neither does Quinn."

Excuse me? I didn't care? I let it go. I didn't want to say anything, not for a long while. It was enough just watching Vincent. He was kind of a genius.

"The chaplain in the joint used to tell me that God hates the sin but loves the sinner. I could never get that."

"Not like God. Just like another human being. We're both human beings, living on the same rock. We can make it easier for each other. That's all I'm after."

Randy took another drag on his cigarette, dropped back his head, and slowly let the smoke escape. I could never have imagined a set of lungs could hold so much smoke. It crawled out of his nose and drifted upward. He opened his mouth and the smoke curled around the corners of his mouth. He didn't speak until all the air had been released, and then he said, "I didn't mean to." Woi Yesus. He's going to confess, I thought, which would make a cop come on a cracker, but it was the last thing Vincent wanted to hear without an attorney present. I expected him to hold up his hands, put on the brakes, call everything to a screeching halt. But he didn't.

"Things got out of hand, the way they do between a man and a woman. You know how it is, signals get crossed. The air ignites, like it was full of fumes."

Vincent sat silently for a moment, then moved his eyes from Randy to the peeling wall.

"Randy, you grabbed her in a parking lot."

"I mean, after that. I mean, you know, when we were feeling each other out. Didn't that ever happen to you?"

"What?"

We were both mystified.

"You're in a car with a girl. You want it to

204

go one way, she wants it to go another. Sparks fly, buttons get pushed . . . things get physical."

"What you're describing, Randy, is a date that went sour. Is that what happened?"

"Something like that."

"No, nothing like that. That's not what this was. And no, that never happened to me, because when I meet a girl I'm introduced or something. I don't grab her off the street. I let her say how physical it's going to be."

True. That one night, I told him, Go for it, knock yourself out. I should care. Back in the day, though, orgasms used to explode all out of me, one after another, five in a row was not unusual, until Connors would say, That's enough for you, and we would both laugh.

"Vincent, you don't fuck a lot of girls, do you?"

"No, Randy, I'm afraid I don't, but that has nothing to do with how you treat another person."

What a conversation for me to be listening to!

Randy Merck smiled his shy smile. "You probably don't even carry a knife."

"No, I don't."

"I always had a knife, even in the joint."

"Well, like most people, I don't carry a knife. Or a gun."

I carry a gun, I wanted to say, and I know how to use it, more or less. Da frick. I dummied up, though. I didn't want to derail what was going on down the track. Let Vincent do that, if he wanted to.

"You two fucked each other, though."

Da frick, again.

"I beg your pardon?" said Vincent.

"Anybody can see that," said Randy. "Don't worry about it."

We were both distracted by his psychosis and his unwelcome insight, but not so much that we didn't realize that Randy had just confessed to murder. Big problem for Vincent. I was glad. At least I wanted to be glad.

"You'll tell all this to Wendy, won't you?" asked Vincent.

"All what?"

"What happened that night, in the car."

"Do I have to?"

"Randy, you are in one of the worst places a human being can be. Since you are, you don't have to say anything. You don't have to do anything. That's the way our system works. On the other hand, you *can* and should tell your lawyer the entire truth. That's the safe and smart thing to do."

206

"This knife you always carry . . . ," I said. Vincent looked at me with a little dismay, but he didn't stop me. "Why didn't you use it?"

"I did. That's how I got her in the car. A blade is a fearsome thing."

"But you didn't kill her with the knife. Why's that?"

Randy had to think for a moment. "Because she was so pretty, I guess. Or just the way things happened. We were parked on this street next to the tracks, down in Sodo."

South of the Dome, which is south of nothing now, since they blew up the King Dome.

"I put the moves on her and she started to fight. I got her into a neck hold and squeezed. I didn't really mean to do . . . what, you know, happened, but I held on so long and so hard . . . She went. I drove around for a while and then stopped, dumped her out. End of story."

"She started to fight?" I asked.

"Yeah . . ."

"She was a strong girl. An athlete. Played soccer and basketball. Was on the swim team." None of this I knew for a fact. I was just trying it on.

"So?"

"You're kind of a small guy." Which is not

the sort of thing you say to any man, I don't care if he's five feet tall.

"I'm about average, but I'm strong. I can whup bigger than me. You're not strong, you don't survive on the yard. You wanna arm wrestle, find out?"

"Maybe later."

"I'm not so small."

"I should have said not so big."

"I got eight inches."

"At least God gave you that."

"Are you finished, Quinn?" Vincent asked, meaning, I hope you're finished.

"It was rush hour," I said. "Weren't you visible to traffic?"

"Nobody cares."

Apparently.

"Vincent, listen," he said, turning away from me, "whatever you want to know about that night . . ."

"I don't want to know *anything* about that night," Vincent said quickly. "You've already told me too much."

"But I wanted to." Randy knitted up his brow and then he looked at me.

"Just one thing . . . you were alone, weren't you?" Vincent wanted to know.

"Yeah, just me 'n her."

"So Mr. Voss is somebody in your head?"

"No, Mr. Voss is out there. Somewhere."

He took the last drag on his cigarette and stepped it out on the floor, even though an ashtray was on the table. "Mr. Voss" — he sighed again — "was a friend of my father. Not a friend, really, 'cause my father didn't have any friends, just people he used. Mr. Voss was one of them. He'd take me to the Sonics games, and then, comin' back to Bremerton on the ferry, he'd . . . do things to me, in the car. When he dropped me off at home, he'd give the old man some money."

"And you were how old, at that time?"

"Eight, nine."

It got worse. As it got worse, Vincent's job would get easier, and since I worked for him things should have got easier all around. What fools we are, ain't?

16

We walked away from the courthouse. I thought we were going back to our offices. I was too turned around to notice we were going in the wrong direction.

"That sorry sack of shit actually confessed," I said.

"That he did."

By now we were going down the hill on Marion, toward Second Avenue.

"You helped him along."

"I did?"

"I could claim you didn't."

"Open to interpretation, always."

"I've never seen you do that before."

"Couldn't seem to help myself."

"You're not trying to make life easier for the mother, are you?"

"Of course not. I wish I could."

The windows of the Metropolitan bar were at foot level. Vincent looked down and scanned the joint.

I realized why we had come this way. I pulled him to the curb. "Forget that woman, Vincent. Whether you led him or not, the kid confessed. You have got to do something about that."

"I'm not sure I do."

"If you don't, I will."

"Like, what?"

"Tell the police. Tell Wendy. The man says he did it."

"But we always knew that, didn't we?"

It was frustrating, sometimes, talking to Vincent. I was still new to the mission. Maybe I still didn't get it. Save the dying, that's all Vincent thought about. Except, of course, for his current preoccupation with the grieving mother of a murder victim, whose murderer had now invested a good deal of trust into Vincent. Me, I didn't know who to trust.

"At least call Wendy."

"I will."

"Now!"

We reached Second Avenue. I tried to steer him across the street and away from the Met, but the light was against us.

He searched his pockets for his cell phone, opened up his briefcase and looked for it there. "I left my phone in the car."

He was forever leaving his phone in the car.

The cell phone in the hands of most people has become primarily an affordable GPS. "I'm on First near Union." "Hi, it's me. I'm on Union approaching Fifth." Let's say the people on the other end *want* to know exactly where this doofus is, and that's hardly a safe bet. What gets my panties in a twist is that *he* really wants people to know where he is, at all times, down to the street corner. As though the rest of the world might miss him if he were out of contact for a minute and a half. Vincent was different with his cell phone. If he left it in the car, nobody had to know where he was.

I gave him mine. "Call Wendy," I rasped.

He looked at his watch.

"Forget it," I said, "they're done with lunch. Call Wendy. Da frick."

He started to dial the number, but I pulled the phone away from him.

"First, where am I supposed to go, and what's it have to do with Wendy?"

"What are you talking about?"

"You and Wendy have some shit errand lined up for me and neither of you wants to tell me what the hell it is."

"Oh, that."

"Yes, that. Before you talk to her about this, talk to me about that." I was sliding into another hot flash and in a moment or two I might become nasty.

"They're going to hang the Fat Man."

"Yeah, I know that."

"Wendy wanted me to go."

"Get out. Why?"

"It's the first hanging in years."

"Yeah? So?"

"Wendy and a bunch of other defense attorneys want me to witness it for them, and the Fat Man doesn't mind. He kind of likes me."

"Why don't she and her gang go themselves?"

"She said they don't want to turn it into a circus."

"The hell. It *is* a circus."

"Truth is, Walla Walla is in the middle of nowhere and they assumed, correctly, that I didn't have that much to do."

"How do I fit in?" I asked, but I already knew. Vincent couldn't do it. He didn't have it in him. Unpleasant experience to be endured? Get Quinn.

"I was hoping you would go for me. Consider it another investigation."

"And what am I supposed to be investigating, watching the Fat Man hang?"

"They're hoping you might see something, something might happen that supports their contention that hanging is cruel and unusual punishment."

"And if you were to see that, it might wreck you, 'cause you're already on the berm, right?"

"I'm a coward. They'll pay you your hourly rate plus fifty percent."

"Sounds like a fun night out, but, you know, I've already seen a couple of people die violently, and they might have even deserved it, but the problem is, once seen, you see it forever, if you know what I mean. Count me out."

"I kind of promised them."

"Da frick. Vincent."

"I told Wendy that I was afraid, but that you were fearless."

"I am."

"I know that. That's why I assured them you could watch it with a cold eye and report back with a clear head."

17

I didn't say yes, I didn't say no. I left him swinging on the hook for a while. Hell, though, I knew I would do it.

We had more pressing things to deal with at the moment. I gave him back the phone. "Call Wendy," I said.

"Shall I tell her you'll go?"

"That's a separate phone call. Tell her Randy just confessed."

He took my phone and dialed.

"It's Vincent. Something kind of accidentally happened during our conversation with Randy, something that has never happened before, with any other client."

"Oh? What's that?"

I had my head next to Vincent's, listening in.

"How much of what passes from your client to me do you want me to pass on to you? Because we never made that clear."

A normal person would say, Everything. A

lawyer would say what Wendy said. "That depends."

"On what?"

"On whether or not it helps me mount a defense."

"He confessed, okay?"

I was relieved that he spit it out, not giving himself the chance to analyze whether this would hinder or help her strategy.

"And knowing this should help me, you think?"

"I would think so, yes."

"You're adorable."

"Had to tell you."

"I suppose you did. My defense remains the same. Randy had nothing to do with this. He was with Mr. Voss and they found the abandoned car."

"Yeah, well, he told me a little about Mr. Voss, too."

"Whoa! That's enough for this conversation, thank you very much. Let's do it this way, Vincent: if I want to know something, I will ask you. Otherwise I don't want to know."

"Are you sure?"

"What's wrong with that?"

"I'd be more comfortable sharing everything."

"I don't need everything."

"If that's the way you want it."

"I think that will work out just fine," she said.

And that was it. He handed back the phone.

"It won't work out just fine," I said.

"It could."

"What if she actually gets him off? Stranger juries have sat."

"That's unlikely."

"You think so? No witnesses, no murder weapon, no DNA. And frankly, look at him. He doesn't look like he could do it."

It's an interesting divergence, between defense lawyer and mitigation investigator. The lawyer wants to get the client off, free and clear; the mitigator only wants to keep the client alive in prison.

Over my objections, Vincent made a quick pass through the Met, looking for his obsession. The sky darkened and the wind whistled down Second Avenue, stinging my face, but I didn't mind that much. I could think about the wind for a moment instead of all the other stuff. I lowered my head and turned my back to the wind.

He came back out and without a word we made our way to the Pioneer Building with the wind pushing us.

18

We opened our raincoats and shook off the rain. I pressed the button for the elevator. The creaky old car came down to the lobby, the door opened, and guess who?

Abby, standing alone.

"I'm sorry I missed lunch," Vincent said.

"Oh . . ."

"Vincent Ainge, from the courthouse?"

"Yes, of course. Excuse me, I'm a little distracted today."

She stepped out of the car and into the small lobby.

"Yeah, so are we," I put in.

"I've never been in a courtroom before."

"Beastly places," Vincent observed.

"We assumed, Arnie and I, that you got tied up, your meeting and everything. Maybe next time."

"Were you up at Arnie's office?"

"Yes. He's been very helpful, if not over-protective. Don't get me wrong, I could use a little protecting, but I am an adult after all."

She buttoned up her raincoat, looked outside.

"Look at it out there," she said.

"Could be one of those years," Vincent said.

There have been years in Seattle where spring never came and summer seemed like fall.

"Are you going back to the courthouse now? I'll go with you . . . if you like."

The guy was gaga. I should care. The elevator had already gone back upstairs. I was wishing I was on it.

"No. To the ferry, back to the island. Arnie wanted me to stay, but I'm tired. I don't want to sit there and have to look at that . . ."

"*Scumbag* works for me," I said.

"I don't want to be in his presence all afternoon. I'll be there often enough, for the trial."

"Are you going to come over here every day?" he asked her.

"For the trial, you mean?"

"Yes, for the trial."

"Yes, every day. I suppose I have to. I'm not looking forward to it."

"What about your husband?"

"Ex-husband. No, he's gone back to Hawaii."

"Hawaii?"

"That's where he lives now."

"Imagine that, living in Hawaii."

"People do."

"Incredible. I've dreamed, once or twice, about going to live in Tahiti. Moorea, to be exact. I must have read about it somewhere."

"What's stopping you?"

"It's not what's stopping me, it's what's propelling me. Which is nothing, apparently."

"And your wife? Is she propelled or stopped?"

"There is no wife. There's an ex-wife. Who's about to become somebody else's wife."

Well, I may have known about the Tahiti dream, but I didn't pay it much mind. The other thing, you'd think he'd have mentioned, ain't? I hated standing there watching this love dance of the injured, and yet couldn't seem to pull myself away.

"Is that difficult?" she asked.

"So far. An older guy. Seems she's been having an affair with him, off and on, since she was seventeen. I should be happy for them that they finally got me out of the way."

"My ex, I learned, has a girlfriend."

"He told you that?"

"Couldn't wait. I didn't like it, either. Funny, huh?"

"Don't worry, you'll soon have a boyfriend."

He made her laugh a little. I thought it was right out of high school, but aren't the early days of love always?

"What makes you think so?"

"You're a beautiful woman, and sweet and gentle."

Now he was embarrassing her. Da frick, he was embarrassing *me.*

She said, "I can't imagine it."

"Yeah, I know. When I have a juicy dream? It's still always with her, my ex-wife. It can be upsetting."

Which was another thing he'd never told me. Before. Not that I should care. Still, in a way I did.

"You're very forthcoming, aren't you?"

"Me? I'm an open book."

"Oh, I suspect you have your secrets."

If she only knew.

"Everybody has secrets."

Tell her, for God's sake, spit it out! But no, not our Vincent.

He said, "So you'll be at the courthouse every day, sitting with Arnie?"

"Suppose so. What can I say? He's attentive."

"Can I walk you to the ferry?" Vincent asked, as though to say, See, I can be attentive, I can be protective.

"Oh, I'll be fine."

"I know, but if you don't mind, I'd like to."

What could I do? I couldn't grab him by the arm and pull him into the elevator, though I sure wanted to. I let him go. I watched him take her arm and walk through the wind to First Avenue, behind the backs of the three Indians who were sitting under the pergola passing a bottle of Thunderbird.

19

At Walla Walla they'd stopped calling him the Fat Man. He was now known as *the ISDP,* which stands for "the Inmate Subject to the Death Penalty." Oh, the game. You've got to know the lingo to know the game.

I'm going to try to keep this brief . . . and I'm going to fail. So I decided to go to the hanging and report back, but before I ever arrived at Walla Walla I'd learned a few things about the process, the rules of the game.

I learned that a trained and certified hanging technician had already made a trip to the local Ace Hardware store, where he purchased with a state Visa card thirty feet of one-inch manila hemp rope. From there he went on to the local Rip 'n Stitch Fabric Shop, where he bought two yards of denim, which his wife fashioned into two matching hoods, one for the condemned, another for her husband.

It didn't have to involve his wife, but that's the way I imagined it happened.

The deal requires two hanging technicians. Together they boiled and stretched the rope. They tied the knot following the regulations put into play by the US Army. When was the last time the army hanged anybody? It had to be an Apache. I'm glad my son is in the navy, anyway.

Those two treated the knot with wax and a dollop of K-Y Jelly, so it had a smooth slipping action. Each time the rope was touched a checklist was initialed. If somebody made a mistake, I imagine, he had to erase his initials and initial the erasure.

Nowadays the trapdoor is activated electronically. A union electrician and an engineer have checked and rechecked that mechanism. Certified it by two sets of initials.

A scale was calibrated and upon it was made to step the ISDP, aka the Fat Man. Still on his diet, he weighed in at 281 pounds. Everybody was thrilled.

An army chart was consulted and it was determined that the optimum drop distance would be five feet even. Anything less and the Fat Man might slowly strangle in the air. Anything more might result in a bloody decapitation. Woi Yesus.

The two technicians measured the Fat Man from his chin to the floor. They did the math to determine the rope length, which equals S minus C plus D, where S represents the scaffold crossbeam height and C represents the Fat Man's chin height and D represents the drop distance. Done and initialed.

They added seven feet to their calculation and cut the rope to size.

They filled two sandbags each with exactly 140 1/2 pounds, both bags making the weight of one Fat Man. They dropped the package a total of twelve times without a glitch. The gallows, the beam, the trapdoor, the rope, all performed as required. Initials were initialed.

Now, throughout the whole process, the Hangman was not consulted or advised. In fact, this fabled dark figure of lore has no training whatever. Nada. His only responsibility is to release the trapdoor when the warden signals him. Which is not to suggest that no qualifications are required. Only those that have to be accepted on faith.

Funny thing: the Fat Man doesn't have to hang. He can go for lethal injection, he can lie down, have a shot, and quietly go bye-bye. Failing to make a choice, however, the default selection is hanging. The Fat Man and all the others waiting behind him were refusing to choose. Their legal position was that it's a Hobson's choice, which in itself is cruel and unusual. They have a point, if you should care, which I don't.

With those special details tucked away in my burning brain, I made the long drive to Walla Walla, a journey not altogether unfamiliar to me. Alone, in my new PT. Two hundred and sixty miles, over the Snoqualmie Pass and down into Ellensburg, over the Yakima Ridge, across Rattlesnake Hills and Horse Heaven Hills into Kennewick, then down into Walla Walla, spitting distance from the Oregon border. By the time I got there I was already beat up, and I hadn't slept well the night before.

I watched the Fat Man make it up the scaffold under his own slow steam, having earlier popped a state Valium. The two technicians Velcroed his legs together. The Fat Man shook his head at the warden's offer to say a few last words, which greatly disappointed the press present. The techs slipped the hood over the Fat Man's head and tightened the noose snugly behind his left ear. They left the stage to two guys in hoods, the Hangman and the ISDP. Only the Hangman's hood had eyeholes.

Okay, I'll admit I twitched when the door

dropped. Try not to. Somehow, I was expecting another moment's interlude or something . . . an extra moment of silence . . . but suddenly the door just fell open and the Fat Man fell behind it. He hung there, turning achingly slowly, this way, then that way, for eight minutes.

We sat. I thought about Randy Merck, because I was watching what I believed would be his sure fate. No way would Vincent save that twisted soul. Then two guards came in from the wings and along with the two techs held up the deadweight until one of them could release and remove the noose. They lay the Fat Man on the floor and removed the hood and restraints, and a doctor pronounced him dead, and that was pretty much it. Thanks for coming.

I didn't know quite what I was going to tell Vincent and Wendy. If the state was determined to do it, then this was as good as anything. It was better than bad liver death, for instance. Better than tying them in a burlap bag and chucking them in the lake.

Did the Fat Man feel any pain? Who can say? If he did, it lasted maybe a second. Did I myself feel diminished, brutalized even? To be honest, a moment after, I was thinking only about the long lonely drive through the night back to Seattle.

When the line of witnesses left the gallows area, I remained seated. I can't say why. Benumbed maybe, still thinking about Randy. The warden gently roused me and said I should go now. He asked me if I was a member of the family. No family members came. Rather than tell the warden the truth, I said I was the mitigation investigator on his case.

He offered me a cup of coffee before I headed out. He seemed a decent guy. I was sure he had duties to attend to, especially at this moment, but he said he had only one more thing to do that night and it could wait. He did not enjoy many of his duties, but he did them well. After half an hour or so, he escorted me out of the prison proper and to my car. By that time the lot was empty. All the press and the chanting crowds for and against had gone home. We shook hands and wished each other a good night, what was left of it. But when I put the car into gear nothing happened. The car wouldn't go forward, it wouldn't go backward. I pressed down on the accelerator, the engine revved, but the car went nowhere. I asked the warden if he knew anything about cars. He looked under the hood. He borrowed my flashlight and lay down on the ground, on his spread-out raincoat. He peered under the car. "I'll be damned," he said. "I've seen it all now," he said.

Somebody had stolen my driveshaft. In the prison parking lot. Right out from under my car.

We talked about how such a thing could have happened, and who would be bold enough to wrench off my driveshaft in all the hoopla of a man being hanged.

There was a Chrysler dealership not too far away, but the warden knew a guy who worked on everything from lawn mowers to semis.

"I could have the car towed to his shop, but it's probably going to be a couple of days before he can get another shaft," the warden said. The Chrysler dealer couldn't do it any quicker, and it would be a lot more expensive.

I thought about how I might fill forty-eight hours, maybe more, in Walla Walla. I asked him about a bus.

"I don't know. I guess a bus goes to Seattle, but not before the morning, most likely. Now, there is a way of getting you back tonight, but . . ."

"There is? That'd be great."

Anything, anyway, I thought. I was desperate not to have to stay in Walla Walla. And so I went with the warden to the loading dock. Remember that one more thing the warden had to do that night?

The coroner's Nissan pickup, the bed covered with a LEER shell, was backed up to the platform. On a stretcher lay the Fat Man in a body bag. The warden unzipped the bag and officially identified its contents. A guard searched it to make sure no one else was in there with the Fat Man, or in the coroner's truck, or under the coroner's truck. The bag was rezipped and they moved what used to be a fat man and now was a dead body into the back of the truck.

The coroner was a man named Raymond Rumble, and he said he would be pleased to carry me back to Seattle, would welcome the company. I shook hands again with the warden and we wished each other a good night, what little was left of it now. I got into the Nissan with the local coroner.

"I'm a little surprised, frankly," said Ray Rumble. The windshield wipers were putting me to sleep, even though the bench seat was far from comfortable. "I figured some court somewhere, like the Ninth Circuit, would put through a last-minute reprieve. I'm only part-time, you know, and the farm don't get put on hold just because somebody in Walla Walla might get hanged at midnight. I was sleepin' in my clothes when they called and said it went down."

"The farm?"

"I farm alfalfa. Got three hundred acres planted."

"You're a farmer?"

"Primarily. Except when they need a coroner."

He was on his way to Harborview Medical Center in Seattle for the official autopsy on the Fat Man, on which he would participate and assist.

"My guess is he died by hanging," said the coroner, deadpan. "I'd like to take a look at his liver, though, all the talk about that. Double dead man walkin', more like it."

He told me that after the autopsy he would have to reload the remains of the Fat Man and take them back to Walla Walla for burial, compliments of the state, since nobody else wanted them.

"How 'bout you? You a lawyer?"

"No, not a lawyer."

"Oh, my, you're not related to . . . ?"

"No, no, no relation."

I guess since we had more time, I told him I was a PI, and I told him how I'd wound up witnessing the execution.

We watched the road unwind and I told him about working in mitigation. I told him about Randy and how he was sure to hang and how I didn't much care but had a hard time picturing him killing someone. The Fat Man, no problem, easy to imagine. Randy, not so easy.

We rode the long dark road. I wasn't on fire, for which I was grateful, but I felt lost in a feverish dream. A dead man was lying in the truck just behind me, after all.

"Would you like me to drive for a while?" I asked.

"I'd like nothing more, but no can do. If anything happens to our friend back there, it better be me at the wheel when it does."

"Looks like the worst has already happened."

The coroner laughed. You can't begrudge a man a laugh, not when he does that kind of work.

We left I-90 at Cle Elum and found an all-night café, part of a gas station. Ray Rumble filled the tank and I made a tunnel around my eyes with my hands and pressed against the shell window to make sure the Fat Man was still there.

Except for two fishermen meeting up for an early breakfast before putting into the Yakima River, we were the only ones in the small café, sitting over coffee and apple pie à la mode.

We left just behind the fishermen, who were checking their tiedowns on the boat trailer just next to the coroner's Nissan. We exchanged a few words with them about the fishing prospects on the Yakima. One of them leaned back against Ray's truck as we chatted, never knowing there was a dead man inside. I told them they had a fine-looking boat, and Ray said the weather looked like it might clear up for them.

Back on the road we lost speed lugging our cargo to higher elevations. The little Nissan made the pass; we hit some snow and rolled down the other side of the Cascades.

You know how sometimes the sun doesn't rise in Seattle, the dark simply lifts? It was that kind of morning. The coroner drove his rig down into the city as though through a color chart, from darker to lighter shades of gray.

He dropped me off at James Street, across the street from the apartment and in front of my office. We shook hands.

"Don't you worry about your car. There's always somebody wanting a ride to Seattle. We'll have it delivered to your door."

I thanked him and instead of walking

across the street went down past the pergola
and the three Indians, still on a drunk.

20

"Chevy Malibu. Boo-hoo."

"Chrysler Town and Country. Boring."

"Whoa! My Range Rover. Get it washed!"

"Cadillac Escalade. Ridin' in style, bro!"

"Jeep Liberty. No comment."

I slowed my pace and went to the curb as though I was waiting for someone. The Indians weren't interested in me. I doubt they could muster one hard-on out of the three of them. These guys were becoming a fixture, part of the neighborhood, and I was goofy enough, after watching a hanging and having my driveshaft ripped off and riding all night with a farmer who happened to be a coroner, to take an interest in what amused my neighbors.

They were identifying makes and models of cars as they passed by, a game I used to play with my old man. The three Indians, as did we, had their favorites and treated others with derision. They fantasized owning their favorites like the old man and I had as we cruised in our Ford station wagon, quite a dandy machine in its own right.

It brought a smile to my lips. After the grimness of the night before, it was a good way to start a new day.

"What the fuck is that?" said one of them.

"Fuck me, dunno."

"Plymouth Prowler," I told them.

"Plymouth? No way?"

"Limited edition. You can probably get a nice one for about twenty-five grand."

"Thank you, ma'am."

"You're welcome."

"Can you help us out with a down payment on one?"

I gave them a five and they professed friendship for life. They scurried up James, heading for the Korean store and some fortified wine. I doubted the store was open this early.

I rang up Vincent from the keypad at the entrance. I woke him up.

"I'm back," I said. "Down on the street."

"How'd it go? What took so long?"

"You wanna get breakfast? Meet me at Larry's?"

Waiting for Vincent, I found I still had in my jacket pocket the small handbook of

Scientific Murder Investigation. I opened it to the section on Ear Witnesses. Three categories: witnesses to things heard before the murder, witnesses to things heard at the time of the murder, and witnesses to things heard after the murder. As for the second group, "Careful inquiry should be made to all things heard by them, such as: . . . outcries, laughter, thud, singing, water running, radio, grating, whistling, dragging object, hammering . . ." and on and on. Me, I could still hear the slow heavy footfalls of the Fat Man ascending the scaffold, the fans in the heater vents, the heavy breathing of the witnesses, the warden asking for last words, the rustle of the hood being slipped over, the drop of the door, the snap of the rope. I could hear all that, and the moments of utter silence that followed.

When Vincent arrived we ordered oversized, high-cholesterol breakfasts and drank cup after cup of coffee. I told him what I'd seen and warned him that I probably wouldn't be working for him for much longer. I needed to find something I could understand. Then I asked him what had happened when he'd walked Abby to the ferry.

"She'd just missed a boat so we had coffee."

"What in the world did you have to talk about?"

"Quite a bit actually. She read me . . ."

"She read you?"

"Little things. Mostly she was wrong. Then I read her. Mostly I was right."

"And you never told her your passion in life, what you do for a living?"

"How could I?"

"How did you leave it?"

"We shook hands at the ticket booth and then I did something dorky."

"No."

"I opened up my arms and asked, 'May I?' "

"I'm relieved. That's not too dorky. What did she say?"

"She said, 'I could use a hug,' and I said, 'Trade you,' and so we hugged."

"Now, that *is* dorky."

"For a moment I was at peace."

"Vincent, I tell you this as a friend and one-night stand: leave the lady alone. No good can come of this. Only pain and heartbreak. She will find out. She has to."

I'd like to say he took my good advice. He didn't. Stupid love.

21

Now that the trial was about to begin, Arnie Stimick called an official meeting of the Friends of Eileen, a brainstorming organizational meeting to prepare for the fight to hang Randy Merck.

I was going to take a pass.

"What else do you have to do?" Vincent asked me.

"Wash my car," I replied, "they brought it back dirty. Looks like they had a sit-down dinner for four in it."

"Even Bernard is going, and he's like a quasi-criminal."

"Then he can tell us what went on, later."

"What about your input?"

"Let it stay put."

"There'll be free food, Cajun style."

"Well, that would usually get me running, but can't you see how it might look? When the truth comes out? If you have to bone this lady, do it once or twice under the radar and dash away, dash away."

"Quinn, Quinn, Quinn . . ."

"Don't Quinn me, I know what this is all about."

"I'm not going to open my mouth. I'm just a warm body, showing a little support by showing up."

"The word *hypocritical* comes to mind."

"Why can't I be a friend of Eileen? The emotion's not hypocritical."

"Then what is it, something about this strikes me as wrong? *Everything* about it strikes me as wrong."

"Look, okay, I don't want Randy Merck to be hanged. I'm going to move heaven and earth to keep him alive. That's what I do. But I do want him boxed up for life. I see that as justice."

"Yeah, yeah, I know all that, but Arnie doesn't and neither will the others. They *do* want him hanged. You should go there and stand up and tell everybody what you just told me."

"I could do that."

"Then I'll go, 'cause I wouldn't want to miss that. I will be armed."

A dozen people showed up and milled together on the open loft of the New Orleans, far fewer than had gathered in the street outside the courthouse that day of the demonstration. The owner of the club contributed the space and some corn fritters and a heaping pot of jambalaya. It was five thirty on a rainy evening.

Vincent and I picked up a pint of Hale's Pale downstairs at the bar before going up to the loft. Arnie was introducing Abby to everybody, a proprietary arm around her shoulders. Bernard waved to us from across the room, calling us over to his side of the loft.

Then Arnie and Abby were moving toward us, splitting us, actually, on their way across the room.

"Hello again."

"Hello, Mrs. Jones," Vincent said, even though he had already put some moves on her. Discreet, he was. He didn't want Arnie to know.

"Oh, I think you can call me Abby."

Arnie left us to welcome the latest arrival, a deputy mayor I recognized. Bernard headed to the buffet for some more corn fritters. I looked at the two of them and decided to do likewise. Loading up my tiny plate, I glanced back at them, in close conversation.

I couldn't help it. I kept watching them. He said something that rattled her. I hoped he was fessing up, but later I learned that he'd told her the only reason he was there was to see her again. Da frick.

Before either of them could recover from his words, Stimick called the meeting to order.

Everyone took seats. Arnie waved Abby to the front row, and Vincent let her go, hanging back to sit in the rear with Bernard and me.

"What was that all about?" I asked.

"I'll tell you later."

Arnie stood before the group and said, "I want to welcome you all here this evening. I know it's the end of the day and you'd like to get home, so I'll keep it brief. Thank you, Gail, for the delicious food and this nice space."

We all politely applauded.

"I think you all know Abby Jones, Eileen's mother."

I was praying Arnie wouldn't ask each of us to introduce ourselves, that sort of thing. I gag on that crap.

"This meeting is about more than one vicious act of violence. It's more than the loss of one beautiful young girl we all held dear, a girl in whose presence we felt better somehow." He was already beginning to tear up. "No, our overriding concern at this point in time, I think, is public safety in downtown Seattle. More specifically, right here in Pioneer Square. This neighborhood is no longer safe, if ever it was."

I thought it was. Relatively speaking. I mean, it's where I live now.

"Granted, it's always been 'colorful' . . ."

He made the finger signs for quote marks. I see somebody do that, I want to break a couple.

"I'm a transplanted New Yorker, as some of you know, and I'm no stranger to groups of harmless boozy raconteurs, et cetera, passing around a bottle and panhandling to get another. These days, though, down here, there's a younger and more aggressive element taking over. This bunch even scares the winos. Small businesses are relocating to Bellevue and Kirkland because their employees and customers don't feel safe in Pioneer Square. The art galleries are suffering. You want to know the county's response? They've offered county employees self-defense courses."

Everybody snorted and shook their heads at the irony.

"And at taxpayers' expense, I might add. I should ask, do any of you live in the neighborhood, or are we all commuters?"

I tried to crunch down in my chair. Vincent stood up and announced, "I live two

243

doors away."

What the hell was this? Was he going to make his announcement, come out, so to speak? Would he tell everybody what he did for a living and that he was on intimate terms with the killer?

"What's your opinion?" Arnie asked him. "And would you introduce yourself?"

"My name is Vincent Ainge." He chuckled, which again kind of seemed like inappropriate behavior. Everyone was turned around in his seat, looking at him.

"Sorry," he said. "I was thinking about how at every night course I ever took I had to say my name and my reason for taking the course. I used to take courses at the experimental college. Music courses, mostly, as I think about it. The electric keyboard, 'Fiddlin' from Scratch,' the harmonica, which, by the way, is said to be the only musical instrument you can comfortably play while in handcuffs. All hopeless, I'm afraid, I'll never make music."

Was he already mitigating for himself?

Now Bernard chuckled. The rest just listened with confused expressions.

"Anyway, my name is Vincent Ainge, and I have an office in the Pioneer Building, like many of you, but I also have an apartment, as I said, two doors away. It's ideal. I don't put five thousand miles on my car in a year. I wouldn't live anywhere else. I don't think I *could* live anywhere else. Sure, it's a little funky down here in the square, and the street people can at times be obnoxious, but there are three live theaters here that don't have to do *Brigadoon* every other year. There are more art galleries than you can cover in a day. The best coffee in the city. The best bookstore."

"Do you feel safe?"

"Do I feel safe? I don't particularly feel in danger."

With that he sat down. Huh? He'd said nothing of any great importance, and he certainly hadn't come clean. As I thought about it, he hadn't said he *would,* he'd said he *could.* Well, he *didn't.* I looked for a way to leave gracefully, but we were on the far side of the loft, away from the stairs. And Arnie was standing with his back to the stairs, blocking the escape route.

A freewheeling discussion followed, of what the group could do to improve the neighborhood, to make it safer, not entirely disregarding Vincent's comments as an insider that it was already a pretty good place to live, but bringing their own misgivings as commuters and shopkeepers. They could demand increased police patrol, they said, and they could push to clean up Occidental Park and the pergola on First Avenue — meaning get rid of my three Indians, who had taken over one of those two camping spots. They could resist any new social services or missions. They could try to regulate the taverns and promote anti-panhandling sentiment. I listened to them come up with these ideas as though they were original and bright, as though no one had ever thought about them before. Strike me dead, Vincent spoke up again.

"There is a Pioneer Square Association that tries to do all that. You can join up with them. They've been at it for ten years."

I know Vincent, he wasn't trying to be a wise guy, but Arnie looked at him as though he might be, pressing his chin between forefinger and thumb.

"I mean, I don't want to discourage anyone," he went on, "but there's no point in duplicating another group's efforts."

Which wasn't what he meant at all. What he meant was that even on urban streets nature will prevail. Get used to it.

To my surprise, Arnie said, "He's right. This group formed spontaneously, out of grief and anger. Grief over the loss of our lovely Eileen, and anger that a vicious, dangerous predator should be allowed on the street. Any street. We can clean up Pioneer Square, but then what? The problems will shift to another neighborhood, then circle around until they come back. The real question is, how do we protect women like Eileen from predators like Randy Merck? I'll tell you how. We take this brutal killing personally. We won't let it slip away. We will confront the city, the county, and the state, and we will demand to know: What went wrong? How did this happen? How can we stop it from happening again?"

It was quite a little speech, inspiring one man in the middle to shout out, "A dangerous predator like that should never have been paroled!"

"At least not without warning," said another, trying to calm down the first one. Others piped in. It struck me as foolish. I was content to sit it out, but Vincent — oh, no — sounded off for a third time.

"As a group, we could press for a better warning system. We could push for a law requiring the authorities to use all means, and all technologies, to warn neighborhoods of sex criminals moving in."

Arnie said, "That son of a bitch should not have been let out of prison in the first place."

"Or he should have been in a hospital,"

Vincent said. "The only problem was that —" He stopped himself but it was too late. The room fell silent, waiting. He couldn't shut up at that point.

"Go on," Arnie said.

A few latecomers arrived at the top of the stairs and waited, not wanting to interrupt. He still could have bailed. He could have said, the problem was that they can't keep criminals on ice because the prisons are overcrowded because of government's irrational mania about drugs . . . or there was no money in the budget . . . or . . . the Constitution does not allow for that sort of punishment. He could have, if he'd thought about it for a minute, made himself seem like just one more man angry with the system. I wish he had. Instead, he told them something he knew and they did not.

"The problem was that Western State Hospital wouldn't take him. He had been there before."

WSH is the psychiatric hospital where all sex offenders are examined before sentencing.

"What do you mean, Vincent?"

"The state had tried to send him to Western for treatment. He had been asking for treatment, begging for treatment. The hospital wouldn't take him."

"Why not?"

He seemed reluctant to say, but he was in too far to skip out now. "They said he was too violent."

Well, that tore it. The latecomers were able to find their seats unnoticed in the rumble that followed this ironic news. Randy Merck was too violent for a psychiatric hospital, so the authorities released him to a halfway house in Pioneer Square, where he killed Eileen at random.

They shook their heads. They could have beat them against the wall and accomplished no more.

In some way I can't fully explain, Vincent was out of control. It was the only time I ever saw him seem to enjoy being the center of attention.

"This is a very dangerous man," he said, "and he knows . . . I'm sure . . . that he is dangerous. And I'm sure he doesn't want to be that way. I mean, who would? He's known it since he was thirteen, and so has the state, for just as long."

Of course, everyone wanted to know how he came by all this information. Now was his chance. He could tell them all the truth and make his case . . . and then run for it. But he wasn't going to do that and risk losing Abby, or lose the chance to have Abby. I jumped in and said, "Vincent's a professional investigator. Investigators know what there is to know. It's our business."

They bought it just like that.

"The state screwed up on this criminal," Vincent said. "He was attacking and raping, serving his time, asking for treatment every time he was arrested and never getting any. They had to know this was going to happen eventually. They had to know, but it was away from them, out of their own four walls, and they washed their hands of Randy Merck, just like everyone he ever knew."

The meeting was expected to last an hour, getting everyone home in time for dinner, but the jazz quintet was already setting up on the stage below and tuning their instruments before anyone realized how long we had been talking.

No one realized that Vincent was doing what came natural: mitigating for the killer, casting some blame on the state without ever excusing Randy Merck for the terrible thing he had done. By then he was moderating the meeting and Arnie was listening. No one was excusing Randy, or even sympathetic to him, but, Vincent told them, we have to take some responsibility for the community in which we live. We have to think new ideas, come up with new approaches to crime, new treatment of criminals, because obviously the old ones aren't working.

Finally Arnie took control again and said, "This has been a terrific meeting. We're really onto something here. We can be a force for public safety in this city and this state. We have to take care of one more piece of business before we can all go home and explain to our families why we're so late. We have to elect officers and a board, but I think we can do that pretty quickly. I nominate Vincent Ainge for president of the Friends of Eileen!"

I thought I'd faint dead away.

A panic came over Vincent's face. After the glow of public admiration, he was awakened to find that he had gone too far.

"I'm flattered, but, sorry, I really can't do it."

"You have to do it, Vincent, you obviously have the feel for it," Arnie said. "We'd all be very grateful."

"Go for it, Vincent," said Bernard, that prick. "Duty calls."

"I really have too many demands on my time . . . and, to tell you the truth, I'm not a leader. I'm a foot soldier. I'll be happy to serve on a committee, but . . ."

"Necessity creates leaders," Arnie said,

and the crowd urged him to make the commitment. Abby looked at him with doe eyes.

"I'm a terrible manager. I mean, without exaggeration. I can't even balance my own checkbook. Really, Arnie Stimick is the best choice for the job. I nominate Arnie Stimick."

But it was too late. They elected Vincent by acclamation.

After, he shook hands, dumbly accepting congratulations. Eventually there he was, shaking Abby's hand.

"Thank you, Vincent. Thank you for everything," she said, and she embraced him, and she kissed his cheek.

Da frick.

People were putting on their raincoats and making their getaways. Arnie came up and said, "You ready, Abby? I'll walk you to the ferry."

"Thanks, but Vincent's already offered."

Did not. And Stimick looked a little ticked off. *He* was supposed to be in charge of Abby. Vincent looked at me and smiled sheepishly. I followed them down the stairs and stopped at the bar for another beer. I could see them leave the club. He held her umbrella for her, creating an intimacy. He held her arm and had to press against her as they walked to the Coleman Dock.

22

Vincent did everything he could for Jon Kutzmann, including shaming his aunt onto the witness stand, where she gave heart-wrenching testimony, if you had a heart to be wrenched, which apparently no juror did. She described a childhood of cruel abandonment, resulting in a withdrawn little boy devoid of self-worth, a child who grew into antisocial behavior, substance abuse, pederasty, and finally murder. Mox nix to this jury. They voted to hang Jon and be done with it. The mystery is not why Jon grew up to be a monster, the mystery is how other children like him do not.

A few of the jurors agreed to stay afterward and talk to Vincent. They were sincere people, exhausted by the duty they had been called upon to perform. This was his practice, to talk to jury members, no matter which way the judgment fell. He needed to learn why they were moved or unaffected by the mitigating circumstances he had presented to them.

"I hated him," said one woman, simply. "It may sound heartless, but I couldn't see this person going on living."

"Did his personal relationship with Jesus mean anything to you?"

"Well, that was a beautiful thing. I think he's gonna need it."

Vincent asked the watercolorist, the lover of rhododendrons, if she hadn't identified at all with Jon's artistic inclinations.

"Collages? Any blithering idiot can do collages."

We went to a Starbucks for lattes and we sat at a table.

He sank into himself a little. A man had just been sentenced to death. Later we would meet with another facing the same possibility.

"You didn't come home last night."

"How do you know that?"

"Vincent. I'm a private eye. And an insomniac, with hot flashes so bad I want to fly out the window. What the hell went on last night?"

"You'll disapprove."

"Duh? I know, but you're going to tell me anyway."

"No, I'm not."

"Yes, you are. You need to."

"Okay. I walked her to the ferry. We talked a little about Stimick. I had the feeling she was uncomfortable with him."

"Da frick. *I'm* uncomfortable with him."

"She doesn't altogether trust him. So I said I didn't, either, but I wasn't one to talk. See, I was looking for an opening, to tell her the truth."

"Probably should have done that before you were elected president of the Friends of Eileen."

"I can't believe that happened."

"We'll deal with that later. You're walking to the ferry . . . ?"

"We dashed across Alaskan Way. I couldn't tell her, or say anything, even if I found the courage, because at the moment I couldn't find the breath. I haven't had to run in ages and I was panting for air as we ran to the gate. We made it just as the last stragglers were boarding. Abby gave the attendant her yellow ticket and stopped just beyond. She turned back, looked at me for a moment, and then said good night. Her voice was plaintive. I knew the next move was mine. So I bought a ticket and took her arm and said I'd ride with her. On a boat, in deep water, I thought I could tell her. Neither of us would have anywhere to run."

"So you told her."

"I told her I wasn't entirely honest with her. I told her I've been opposed to capital punishment all my life."

"Good start."

He would have told her the whole truth then, he insisted. He would have told her exactly what he did for a living, that Randy Merck was a client he was pledged to save from the gallows. But at that moment the boat's horn sounded five short blasts, and the passengers all hurried to the forward end, running past them.

"What's that?" he'd asked.

She had been counting the blasts beginning with the third. "Emergency. We're about to run somebody down."

They followed the others, running to the forward end and out onto the weather deck, cold and wet, and there in the water dead ahead was a sailboat, under sail, thirty feet in length, lolling about in the path of the mammoth ferry, soon to be crushed unless it could get out of the way, because the ferry was too big to stop or turn.

"Yachter," someone spit out with disgust.

"He thinks he's got the right-of-way, the asshole," said another.

"Who would be out sailing on a night like this?" Vincent asked them.

"Drunks."

The huge vessel reversed its powerful engines and sounded another five blasts.

"Wastin' your breath on him," said the first man. "He don't know what five horns means."

"Serve 'im right if he's munched," said the other.

Vincent stood at the rail and helplessly watched, holding his breath.

The ferry put the engines forward again and turned hard to starboard. The sailboat turned hard to its starboard. It missed the bow by feet and only inches by the time it cleared the stern. The sailboat got bounced around violently in the wake. They watched it until it disappeared into the darkness and all they could see was its mast light.

When they went back inside, Abby took his hand and led him to seats at the forward windows. They sat and watched the lights of the houses on Rockaway Beach glow brighter as the boat approached the island. Then it made the turn into Winslow and the dock, blasting its horn one long to announce its arrival.

They never picked up the thread of their conversation.

"You spent the night."

"It went in a different direction, the talk."

"I'm sure."

"I think I love her."

"What if she loves you?"

"Is that possible?"

We went across the street and bought Randy a burger and a large Coke. On our way back to talk to Randy, I gave Vincent three little words to remember. By the time the interview was over neither one of us could remember a single one.

Randy all but recoiled at the smell and notion of a hamburger. Turns out our killer was a devoted vegetarian. He fell upon the Coke, though.

I sat on the windowsill, my back against the bars, and ate the burger myself. Vincent and Randy sat on either side of a scarred metal desk in the King County Jail.

"When you're with a girl, and she says no, what do you do?" Vincent asked him.

"I don't give her a chance to say no."

The defense lawyer isn't there when Vincent does his interviews. He never uses written questions or a tape recorder. He tries to make it seem like a normal conversation. He does take notes but that's about it. I don't even do that. I sit and listen. Once in a while, I can't help myself and I'll ask a question, but neither of us ever makes a judgment.

Randy was calm and cooperative and way insane, but in the state of Washington insanity almost never wins as a mitigating circumstance. No matter how whacked out the perp, if he knows, This is my ass, this is my elbow, then he knows, This is right, this is wrong, and he is legally responsible for his acts. Randy for sure knew that killing Eileen was wrong, no matter what whirlwinds churned inside his own sick brain.

"What's your favorite sexual position?"

I was guessing up the ass. I was right.

"Why is that?"

"You fuck a girl up the ass, she'll never forget you."

"She won't?"

"Never."

Considering how many times he himself must have been fucked up the ass, in prison and out, one must believe he spoke with some authority.

"But didn't you want them to forget you, not call the police?"

"Not call the police, but not forget me. I wanted 'em to never forget me. I wanted to be in their nightmares."

"Like Mr. Voss is in yours?"

Randy looked wounded. Vincent quickly changed directions.

"Did you have any childhood heroes?"

"Heroes?"

"People you wanted to be like."

Randy thought about it for a long moment, as though childhood was a concept that had long ago been proven bogus. "I didn't know anybody I ever wanted to be like."

"No teacher or coach, no athlete or movie star?"

"Teacher?"

"Anybody. The president of the United States."

Randy laughed.

"All right, well, back in your cell, why don't you give that some thought. Think about who you might admire."

"Okay, Vincent, I'll do it for you. I'll think of somebody, I promise."

"Now, Randy, before you attack a woman . . ."

"What?"

"Before you attack a woman, you stalk her, don't you? You stalk her for some time. You notice somebody on the street and then you follow her."

"Which woman?"

"Any woman."

He contemplatively tugged at his chin. "I follow somebody around, yeah. You have to."

"What draws you to her?"

"What do you mean?"

"Is it her long hair, her boots, the way she walks?"

"I don't know. Sometimes it happens quick. Everything's right. Bang. But usually I spend some time. I want to see what I'm getting into."

As he spoke, Randy stared at Vincent with a kind of curiosity.

"What emotions do you feel when you're stalking a woman?"

"What do you mean?"

"How do you feel?"

"About what?"

"When you pick a woman, at random, one out of a crowd on the street, and you're drawn to this particular one, and you follow her, are you excited, scared, ashamed? What?"

"Excited. Like in a game. A buzzer goes off, the game begins. You see her, figure she's the one. You follow her. One thing leads to another. It just happens. Sure, it's exciting. It's a special day."

"You know you're going to hurt her?"

"You never know nuttin'."

"You don't know?"

"Go with the flow."

"It's going to lead to violence, you're aware of that?"

261

"Doesn't have to. Usually does."

"Do you ever see her as a person?"

"How do you mean?"

"Well, do you wonder, is she married, does she have children, is she someone who works hard to make her way in life?"

"I don't think of any of that shit." Then Randy stared at Vincent coldly and asked, "Do you?"

"Pardon?"

"You don't want to find out about me, you want to find out about *you*."

"I've never hurt a woman in my life."

He smiled. "Once you start following her, you already hurt her."

I'd hate to think I'm slower than Randy, but I was a big click behind on this. Maybe he had some kind of detector the rest of us don't.

"Her space ain't her own anymore. Her safety shield is broken. Her sassiness don't count for shit. She thinks she's got the world by the tail, but you got her in your sights, you got *her* tail. You liked it, too, didn't you?"

"It was research, ten minutes or so, then I walked away."

Randy cracked up. Laughed until he choked.

"Research, my ass!"

Vincent looked over to me, as if to say, You know me. I was wondering if anybody ever really knows anybody else. Truly, I was dumbfounded.

"I was trying to understand what motivates you . . . and others . . ."

"Yeah, yeah, yeah," Randy said impatiently, "but where did you grab her?"

I couldn't finish the burger. I rolled it up in its wrapper and tossed it into the wastebasket. I was glued to the windowsill, falling deep into another flash, tingling right down to my toes and on the verge of a scream.

"I never grabbed anybody."

Randy's prescience was rattling Vincent. Not to mention me. I wanted him to end the interview.

"Who knows, next time you will bring it to the next level."

"It's not illegal to follow a woman, just to follow."

"All right, Vincent!"

They were now members of the same lodge. Randy put up his hand for a high five. Vincent ignored it.

Me, I passed my fingers across my throat. Stop. Uncle.

Vincent called in the guard and we stepped out into the hall.

23

"Da frick, Vincent! You gotta talk to me."

"Don't get worked up. It was an aberration."

"Just tell me what and why."

I found it hard to stand still. I paced in narrowing circles.

"I was walking north on Fourth Avenue. I was in a brain cramp, an emotional no-man's-land. I stopped at the intersection, because I forgot where I was going. Thinking back, I *still* don't remember where I was going. I tried to get my bearings, waiting for something to come back to me. In the meantime, I happened to see this woman turn down Cherry Street. She caught my eye. Not like you think. Anyway, I followed her."

"Yeah. Why?"

"I was in Randy's head. I thought, if I were a stalker, a predator like Randy Merck, I would myself pick out a woman like this one, a woman in boots, in a short skirt over black leggings."

"Da frick! And you followed her?"

"I don't know why. I'd never done anything like that before. She was attractive. She wore her hair long, rich and brown and falling over a fawn-colored leather jacket."

"Listen to you. You're going poetic."

"I'm describing her. She was only around twenty-five, but sure of herself, in control. I think that's what attracted me."

"Attracted you? You were stalking her! You didn't go up to her and say, Excuse me, I couldn't help noticing the way your long, rich brown hair falls over your fawn-colored leather jacket, and I'd just like to make your acquaintance."

He was creeping me out. He waited for more of my, what, sarcasm? Disapproval, for sure, which might come soon in the form of a punch to the gut. Where's the mitigation, boy?

"For three blocks I followed behind her. She walked up First and went into that little drugstore on Marion. I went across the street and waited. When she came out I followed her up First until she went into the museum, and then I realized I was in a bad dream."

"Or else you realized that museums bore you."

"No, woke up. Why would I want to emulate a stalker? What could I learn from that?"

"That's what I'm saying."

"So I turned around and walked back to the office. End of story."

"That's it?"

"The whole thing. How he could divine that I'll never know. Does it come off on you? Does it leave a smell, a stain?"

"What kind of research was that? That wasn't research."

"No, I know that, it was craziness."

"You told Randy it was research."

"I was only trying to understand. It doesn't matter what I tell Randy. But I'd like you to understand."

"I can't understand something like that, like stalking. You're either into it or you're not, and if you are, you're a sick fuck, which I never thought you were."

"I'm not. You know me better than that. Really, don't worry about it. I'm fine. It was five minutes of craziness, which I recognized as craziness."

"It's not a good sign, though."

"It's over. It was a weird moment and it's over."

I stopped my pacing, and I had nothing more to say.

"Now," he said, "I have to go back and talk to Randy. I have a hunch about something. You don't have to come if you don't want to."

No way was I not going back in there with him.

"I'm coming with you."

"I have to ask him about something. You might not want to be present."

"About what?"

"I have a hunch."

"Again, about what?"

"I think he's done this before."

"We know that. Starting when he was thirteen."

"I mean murder."

Back inside the room, with the guard outside again, Vincent stood behind his chair, his hands on the back of it. I was flashing hot again and had a little trouble breathing. I wiped my face with a Handi Wipe, ran it over the back of my neck, where I expected any moment a fissure to open and lava to pour out. Vincent leaned on his chair for support. He was going to go where he had no right or duty to go.

Randy was slurping the last of his Coke, shaking down what was left of the ice.

"Was Eileen the first girl you ever killed, or were there others?"

Even Randy looked at him as though the question was out of bounds. He looked at Vincent for a long moment, a perverse neediness in his eyes, and then let his head drop.

"Randy?"

He took some more time, looked up again. "Who do you have in mind, Vincent?"

"No one. I'm not talking about any particular case."

"Oh. I thought there was someone . . ."

"I only want to know, for myself, if you ever did it before."

Calm and thoughtful, Randy said in a low voice, "I might have."

"When?"

"I'm only saying I could have."

"You could have?"

"I would have been able to."

"What does that mean, exactly?"

"If the situation popped up, you know, then I might have done it."

"Done what?"

"What you're talkin' about."

"What am I talking about?"

"The thing. You know."

"Have you done it? That thing?"

"I could have."

"More than once?"

"Maybe."

"More than twice?"

"Maybe."

"Would you have told someone about it?"

"I would have kept it to myself. Only stupid people brag. That's how they get caught."

"What would it feel like?"

"Keeping it to myself?"

"Okay. That."

"I can keep a secret. Man, can I ever keep a secret. My old man was puttin' it to me and I kept the secret. All that other stuff, I kept it all to myself."

"Once done, how long before you would think about doing it again?"

"The next full moon."

Vincent's eyes widened, and Randy laughed at him.

"I'm messing with you!"

"About everything?"

"No, just the full moon."

Vincent came around from the back of the chair and sat down. He was tense and weary at the same time.

"So if you had done it before, you might have thought about doing it again, but not necessarily actually do it again?"

"You're losin' me now, brother."

"You might think about doing it again but not actually go through with it."

"I could've done it again. If the situation popped up again in the same way. It might have been me who done it."

"Done what?"

"What you're talkin' about."

"Everyone's wondering about all those prostitutes missing, the ones up on Aurora Avenue?"

"Prostitutes. Nothing but trouble."

"Did you ever stalk a prostitute out on the SeaTac Strip?"

"I've been there a few times."

"Or up on Aurora Avenue?"

"Aurora? Been there lots of times."

"Did you ever kill one of them, one of those women, at either place?"

"You're talkin' about all the whores, right? The killed whores?"

"Yes, I'm talking about them. Prostitutes. Mostly. Not all of them."

"Could've happened thataway."

"They call that killer the Aurora Slasher. Do you know why?"

"They like to give names like that. Remember the Green River Killer?"

"Because he used a knife. He slashes his victims."

"Well, yeah, I could figure that out."

"Are you the Aurora Slasher?"

"Why would I tell you, Vincent?"

"Because you trust me. Because I'm going to make a difference in your life. Because I'm your life ring."

"Maybe I do, maybe I don't."

"What?"

"Trust you. I'm not used to havin' a whole lot of trust in anybody."

"Did you ever kill a woman in any other city?"

"I've been around."

"Like where?"

"Oh, here and there. Portland, Spokane, Reno, Sacramento, Boise."

"Did you stalk and kill women in all those cities?"

"I've been in those cities. I could've done most anything."

"With Mr. Voss? Was Mr. Voss with you?"

"Mr. Voss . . . sometimes he's just in my head."

"Is he with you now?"

"Now? Oh, you mean in my head. No, not now. Maybe tonight."

"Maybe it was Mr. Voss who killed women in all those cities."

"Mr. Voss likes little boys."

"So it was you alone?"

"What I do, like that, I do alone. I'm the

lone wolf."

"Randy, do you enjoy hurting people? Seeing them frightened, seeing them suffer?"

I could tell he'd been asked that before. He had a quick nonanswer. "It all depends."

"Do you enjoy sex, Randy? Sex with a woman?"

"Not all of it. I still have a lot of pain down there."

"Down where? You mean, in your penis?"

"In my scrotum, and in my rectum."

"Why do you have pain in your scrotum and your rectum?"

"Because of all the needles he stuck there when I was a kid."

24

Outside on the street, I told Vincent to get my hair.

"Huh?"

"Hold back my hair, will you, I think I'm going to puke."

I was clutching the head of a parking meter, bracing myself, ready to hurl. It had been a long time coming, starting when I interviewed Randy's father, and now I wanted it, thought I deserved it, but finally was unable to spew it out.

Vincent patted my back and said, "Sometimes at the end of the day I put a pillow over my head and try to hide, but, hey, that's life. It's a bad deal but it's all we got."

I tried to shake it off, hold my mud. "What now?"

"You know I don't cross lines. I stay within the boundaries."

"I used to be that way."

"I've worked in some form of civil service

most of my adult life. Even now, I believe that I am serving the public good. Truly."

"Yeah, I know that."

"I respect and obey the limits of my own job description."

"Where the hell are you going with this?"

"Any action is Wendy's to take."

"Then let's go give her a kick in the ass."

We did.

We told Wendy first about the pins and needles that Randy's father had inserted into his bottom.

She pursed her lips and nodded. Like, Do I need to hear this?

"His father used to push them in and pull them out again. That was his game. Perverted acupuncture. Only sometimes he pushed them in too far and when he couldn't get them out he would just leave them there. You ought to order up some X-rays."

She nodded again. Did I sense some resentment? She turned to me. "Who have you found?"

"I talked to a couple of his old teachers, neighbors. Dear old Dad."

"Did the neighbors love him? Did his teachers?"

"They didn't hate him. Most of them thought that Randy was one strange little boy, but not evil or even violent by nature."

"He was raised to it," said Vincent. "If the state had given him a little help when he first cried out for it, from his first offense, when a little help might have gone a long way, he might have turned out differently. Had they helped as well as punished that boy, Eileen might be alive today."

"Hello? Mighta, coulda, woulda? Stay focused, buddy." This from Wendy.

"I can't help imagining."

"Imagine this: you never have to testify."

"Why not?"

"Because he's acquitted."

"I've never considered that a possibility."

"It's a circumstantial case at best. Where are the witnesses? No murder weapon? Where's the DNA connecting our boy with the victim?"

"Washed away, I would guess, by the heavy rain that fell on Eileen's body all that time."

"I like my chances here. I think I can win this."

Which is about where Vincent decided to cross the line, to step out of his job description. Truth is, it started when his questioning of Randy went beyond the scope of mitigation. Or when he stalked a perfect stranger just to see how it felt. He insisted such a thing had never happened before. Could I believe him?

"Wendy, I won't go into details unless you ask me to, but when I talked to Randy, I got the impression, a strong impression, that he had done this before. Quinn can back me up."

She looked at me. But I didn't back him up. I shrugged. I wasn't sure of anything anymore.

"It's my position," she said, "that he hasn't done anything more serious than joyriding, so forget about what may or may not have happened before."

"I think he's murdered before. There were more —"

Her hand shot up, stopping him.

"Don't say another word, Vincent."

"He may be a serial killer."

"What the fuck did I just say?"

"I'm sorry, I have to tell you. You're an officer of the court."

"Whatever I've already heard from you is secondhand, which I can choose to ignore. Now shut up."

"So we're fired?" he asked hopefully.

"You are not fired. We owe it to the client to be prepared for any outcome. You dig down and find more reasons for keeping this creep alive."

25

It was dark, my wipers on intermittent, when I pulled into the parking lot of Clinton's rest home. I'd been, up to that time, trying to shake off the image of Vincent stalking some unaware girl up First Avenue for no apparent reason, or for a reason he wouldn't or couldn't share with me. Which doesn't explain why I wound up at the rest home, unless I was already trying to mitigate for his behavior, if not for his crime. The old man was losing all his memories but maybe I could shine a light on some dark recess and find what was missing in my knowledge, carnal type aside, of my friend and one-night lover.

As often happens, I went looking for one thing and found another.

I went through the deserted lobby to Clinton's wing, stopping at the nurses' station. The woman on duty knew me from previous visits with Vincent and may have thought I was a family member. I asked her if it was too late for me to say good night to Clinton Ainge.

"I think he's still awake. A volunteer is in there reading to him."

I thanked her and walked down the quiet corridor to his room. His name was in a slot on the door. The slot for his roommate's name was blank, meaning Clinton would be getting a new one soon, meaning the old one had gummed his last applesauce.

I put my ear to the door and heard a female voice reading:

"O Rose, thou art sick!
The invisible worm,
That flies in the night,
In the howling storm,

"Has found out thy bed
Of crimson joy:
And his dark secret love
Does thy life destroy."

Woi Yesus.

Weeks later, I blew half a day Googling and running down an English professor from Seattle University to find out that the poem was called "The Sick Rose" by William Blake. I could have asked the volunteer at the moment and saved myself the aggravation, but that didn't occur to me when I walked into the room and saw that the volunteer was Darla, Eileen's roommate.

She was reading from a well-worn paperback that had clipped to it one of those mini lights. The room itself was in darkness, except for what outside light came through the window curtains. Clinton was in bed, asleep as it turned out, and Darla was sitting at his bedside, with her book, and smoking a cigarette. She tried to palm it when I came inside, and when it became clear that I wasn't going to turn around and leave, she took it into the little bathroom and dropped it into the toilet, without flushing.

Déjà vu for me and you. See, poetry is everywhere.

I'm sure she thought at first that I was the attendant, then probably a daughter, and finally, resuming her chair, she took a moment to actually look at me and say, "Huh? Aren't you . . . ?"

"Quinn. Wuzzup, Darla?"

Clinton snored drily.

"What are you doing here?" she asked me.

"You first."

"I'm here two, three nights a week, reading old folks to sleep. They like it."

"You know this guy?"

"Sure. Clinton. He's one of my favorites. I like the feisty ones. God, he's not your father, is he?"

The lady who comes into his room at night. Quite a coincidence. Or maybe not.

"No, he's not my father, but I know his son."

"Vincent? Small world."

"Yeah, but I wouldn't want to have to rake its leaves. You know Vincent?"

"Not really. I met him once. But he's the reason I'm here, really, reading these guys to sleep."

"And a good job you're doing. He's out. Let me walk you to your car. Unless you've got somebody else to read to."

"No, I always save Clinton for last."

Out in the parking lot she leaned against her little black Geo and lit up another cigarette.

"I thought you didn't smoke."

"I do, though. Too much."

"That night in your apartment, I saw a cigarette in the toilet." Just like the one floating right now in Clinton's toilet. "But both you and Guy said you didn't smoke."

"I was lying. Guy is death on smoking. Funny, huh, him being a rocker and a stoner and everything. So both Eileen and I used to hide it from him."

How do you hide smoking? Especially in your own house. You can smell it on a person. But I wasn't so much interested in that as in her connection to Vincent.

"Eileen and I volunteered on the island while we were in high school. Walking dogs for the shelter and cleaning up. So we wanted to do something in the city. This time with people. We're good girls. Really, we are. Or . . . Eileen was . . . and I still am."

She said it like a mitigating factor, like she had to prove it somehow. I could care less about her virtue.

"Okay."

"And Clinton's son suggested to Eileen that we could read to the old people."

"Say what?"

"We didn't know much about old people but we liked to read, we used to read to each other, so . . ."

"Vincent suggested to Eileen?"

"And she told me. We do it as a team, volunteering. We did everything as a team."

She was trying to tell me one thing, I was trying to get at something entirely different.

"How long have you been doing this? When did you and Eileen start?"

"Six months, more or less."

Vincent had told me he met Eileen about a month before she disappeared.

"And you met Vincent where?"

"Here. At the rest home. Just once. And then he called me once and told me to knock off smoking in the room. I don't know how he knew. Why?"

"And Eileen? How well did she know him? Did she talk about him?"

"No. Just when she told me this man had given her an idea for volunteer work. We knew he was Clinton's son, so once in a while we'd ask Clinton how his son was, but most of the time he was confused about even having a son."

I was a little confused myself. About one thing, though, I was sure: people do good deeds for a variety of reasons, not always charitable. Sometimes they do them to atone for bad deeds, sometimes out of guilt. I was thinking of Vincent, of course, but what I had sensed earlier from Darla came back to me now. She, too, was feeling guilty about something.

"Darla, why would it bother you if Guy knew you smoked?"

"Well, both Eileen and I . . ."

"But he was Eileen's boyfriend, not yours. Wasn't he?"

"Yes, they were boyfriend-girlfriend . . . kinda."

"Were you having a thing with Guy?"

She wanted to tell me. It wasn't coming easy, and why should I care? Still, she needed unburdening.

"Are you feeling bad about that, now that Eileen is dead?"

"How do I explain it?"

"Any way you want to, dear."

"Some people . . . don't understand. They're judgmental."

"Well, I'm not one of those people."

Teenage love affairs. I should care.

"We were in love."

Yeah, yeah. Like, I didn't already get that.

"It happens," I said, sounding motherly despite myself.

"I mean, we were *all* in love. All with each other."

And that's where it got interesting.

"Okay," I said. "How does that work?"

"I was in love with Guy, and Guy was in love with Eileen, and Eileen was in love with me, and I was in love with her, and Guy was in love with me, and Eileen was in love with Guy."

That pretty much covers the waterfront.

"It's called a threesome," I pointed out.

"No, it's called a relationship. We were all

in love, with each other. We dreamed of getting married that way, having children, everything."

"Sweetheart, that wasn't going to happen."

"We couldn't even tell anybody. You know how people are."

"Judgmental, yeah."

She threw away the cigarette and brought a hankie to her eyes.

Look at me, I'm giving her a hug, patting her back.

"And now she's gone," Darla wept into my shoulder.

"It's just you and Guy now."

"It's not. It's not anything. Without Eileen, it's nothing. It's . . . nothing."

In the parking lot, in the night, in the drizzle, I held her as she cried. I marveled at the turns the human heart can take. Ain't?

26

Randy blew smoke rings up toward the flaking ceiling. Inside the King County Jail it was almost as chilly and colorless as the morning outside. He had wolfed down the grilled cheese Vincent brought him and was now sucking on the remains of the Coke.

Vincent asked him about his boyhood. Did he participate in sports?

"Does shootin' pool count?"

The Little League was for chumps. AYSO soccer made no sense at all. I threw him a curve.

"Does the name Carol Christensen mean anything to you?" I asked him.

The sequence of smoke rings went unbroken.

We'd done a little research and committed to memory some of the names and likenesses of the murdered prostitutes. No problem, because the local papers had given the Aurora Slasher rivers of ink. As each missing prostitute was found dead in a Dumpster along some stretch of Aurora Avenue or the SeaTac Strip, her picture would appear in the paper, usually a mug shot from a previous arrest, with muddy contrasts of black and white, unhappy meth expressions, stringy hair, their entire stories right there on their grim faces.

"It might. What's the name again?"

"Carol Christensen."

"It might just ring a little bell. I could of run into a person with that name."

"On Aurora Avenue?"

"Could of been there."

I wanted to smack him upside the head. But we should not have been asking him those questions in the first place. It was, for us, forbidden territory. We were sounding a lot like cops and he was stitting there without a lawyer.

"What about Mary Meechan? You ever hear of her?" I asked. "Could of, might of, maybe . . ."

"It's possible I heard that name somewheres."

"She was the pregnant one."

"That so?"

"Julie Talbot?" asked Vincent. "Ever hear of her?"

"Rings a bell."

"Bottle blonde, petite, about twenty-four?" I prompted.

"Twenty-four, twenty-five."

"A prostitute."

"Those little girls do get into trouble, peddlin' their asses that way."

"Did you kill Julie Talbot?" I asked him. I was working hard to hold my mud. I had a lot going on in my head. I wanted to pop him one.

He turned to Vincent. "Do you want me to say yes?"

"Only if it's true."

"What's true depends on who's tellin' the story, and why, and who he's tellin' it all to. Could be nothin' is true. Could be everythin' is."

"What does that mean?"

"Damned if I know!"

He laughed out loud.

"So you might have killed her? That might be true?" I said.

"There's always that possibility."

"No, Randy, there isn't that possibility."

I jarred him out of his smugness.

"There isn't?"

"No, because Julie Talbot was murdered while you were in the joint. So you're either jerking our chains here or bullshitting Vincent and me for attention, or . . ."

Or maybe the sick shit has racked up enough for an extended stay in hell but not for permanent residence. Maybe he never killed anybody.

"Or?"

"You tell me."

"Or I've killed so many women I can't remember 'em all."

"Which is it, Randy?"

"What difference does it make?"

"To you and to us, not a bit," said Vincent, "but to all those familes and friends still in the dark, it makes a big difference. The difference between knowing and not knowing what happened to a loved one."

"Well, see, that don't cut it with me. Where's Mr. Voss? Dead? Alive? In my head? I don't know. If I knew, then I'd know. Since I don't, then I don't."

"Is Mr. Voss a loved one? Nothing you've said would make me understand that."

"I'll put it this way, he's all I got."

"Well, I'm not talking about Mr. Voss, I'm talking about people and their daughters. Those girls weren't always crack whores or meth messes. Once they were somebody's pride and joy. They were part of a family and they were loved."

Randy laughed out loud.

"Do you enjoy this, Randy?"

"What, talkin' to you? Yeah, I do, Vincent. You crack me up."

"Your life? The whole process? The crime, the arrest, the trial, the stretch in prison, that whole repeating pattern. You like it all, don't you?"

"That's a funny question. The joint's okay. It's an interesting lifestyle, once you learn the ins and outs."

"One way or the other, that's over now, Randy. You've been caught for the big one, murder. No more in and out. You're either in to stay or swinging at the end of a rope. You do understand, don't you, that you're never going to get out of jail again? And that's the best-case scenario. You do understand you might even hang."

Randy thought about those options.

"Do you want to hang?"

"How bad can it be?"

I could have regaled him with the process but chose not to.

"If you do have to spend the rest of your life in prison, how will you live it?"

"Dunno."

"Well, think about it."

"Okay, this has been a lesson to me."

"That's very constructive thinking, Randy."

"Are you fuckin' with me?"

"Are you fuckin' with *me?*"

"I'll stop if you stop."

"You want to get serious?"

"Yeah."

"If you really did kill those other girls, and if you were willing to tell the DA, show him where and everything, I think he might make a deal."

"I thought you wasn't any lawyer."

"You'd have to talk to Wendy."

"Hmmmm . . . I don't think she likes me."

Randy lit another cigarette. Vincent had bought him two packs of Salems, out of his own pocket. I looked at him blowing smoke rings and knew that he was capable of unspeakable things, but could he crush a woman who was fighting back? He couldn't me, that I knew for sure, and I had twenty years on him.

"You know, I've gotten to know Eileen's mother," said Vincent.

An understatement.

"The mother of the girl you murdered?"

"Yeah?"

"You've pretty much ruined her life."

"Shit happens."

"Not by itself." Randy didn't answer. "She'll never live another day without pain, because of what you did. Okay, the pain's inevitable, but the suffering isn't. The damage you've done, Randy, you have no idea, but there's still time to ease the suffering, hers and your own, because we both know you are suffering. You're suffering with the rest. Look at your life. It's horrible. What is it but pain and suffering? You've got so much pain inside yourself you want to spread it around, like a good person who has love inside of him wants to spread it around. But you can end all that, just by taking responsibility for what you've done."

Randy held his head, the cigarette between his fingers releasing smoke in a lazy stream.

"I'm not proud of the stuff I done. Honest. Sometimes I just get out of control, especially when I'm alone with a woman. I'm like, like, a . . . a kitchen match . . . scratch me against the right surface, I light up. You know what I mean? I never wanted it to be that way."

"You can end it, here and now. You can do the right thing. You can still make a contribution to society."

"How, Vincent? What can I contribute? I'm a lowlife, always have been."

"Oh, you know, Randy. You've always known. You just have to find the will, end this bubble of misery that surrounds you, put down the weight you've been carrying, do the right thing . . ."

I hated his words, hated him for hammering them at the kid, but I held my tongue. I knew Vincent thought if he could convince Randy there was value to the rest of his life, and convince him enough to take responsibility for his past life, then convincing the jury would be easy — or better yet a deal could be made. The more Randy was affected by Vincent's words, the harder he pushed him. He was like a charismatic evangelist, drunk on his own talent to inflict shame and self-loathing.

Later that afternoon we got the results of the X-rays Wendy had ordered up for Randy. Eighteen needles were still embedded in his flesh, along with fragments of others that had deteriorated over the years.

27

Since we were with Randy, I never had the chance to bring up my bumping into Darla and the things she'd told me, including the things that were inconsistent with what Vincent had said, and after we left Randy I made a quick getaway. I needed more time to think.

I didn't see him again until Thursday, the first day of Randy's trial.

Local news crews and their cameras lined one corridor of the King County Court-house, electrical cords snaking the hallway. Television equipment was not allowed into the courtroom itself. As Vincent and I walked toward the TV crew, they picked up their cameras and started shooting. For an unsettling moment I thought we were the story. It was an odd sensation and it made me stop in my tracks. Vincent ran into me from behind. When I turned, I saw the bailiff leading Randy, hands cuffed behind him.

"Hey, Vincent. Quinn. Thanks for coming," said Randy, smiling brightly. "Big day."

The newshounds went wild for the smile. They love shooting smiling perps. The press called out their usual breathless questions but Randy ignored them, and the bailiff did not let him break stride. They turned back to us and asked us who we were, but we didn't tell them.

We were electronically searched before we could enter. I wasn't packing anyway. I don't always, and when I don't I wonder if this will be the day I wish I had.

Inside, Randy and Wendy were conferring head-to-head. The judge had not yet entered. The room was deathly quiet. When I opened the door, everyone turned. Several Friends of Eileen were there. They nodded to Vincent, their president.

Abby and Stimick were together and had saved room for us. She waved us over. This time we sat with them and waited. Any kind of talk was impossible, and I was grateful to hear the call, "All rise!"

I saw Abby's eyes boring a hole in Randy's back. Vincent looked straight ahead, his arm pressed against her body.

"Mr. Merck, how do you plead?"

There was that heavy silence, until Wendy nudged him to speak.

He stood up and cast an over-the-shoulder glance at the spectators. He found Vincent, smiled, then turned back to the judge. "Guilty, Your Honor."

First, the stunned silence, then the spontaneous cheer. Arnie was on his feet, punching his fist into the air. The judge pounded his gavel and called for order. Wendy was yanking Randy's sleeve, clutching his arm, that look of horror on her face. "Your Honor. Your Honor . . ." she stuttered.

"And I request the death penalty," said Randy. "No, sir, I'm *demanding* it. The sooner the better. Let's get it over with."

Everyone cheered again. It was a little off-putting, the bloodthirst of the crowd.

I felt Vincent's body move and then saw him rising from his seat and taking the few steps to the defense table. I assumed he wanted a quick word with Wendy, but instead he spoke out, silencing the crowd. "Your Honor . . ."

A great confusion swept over the spectators. Me? I had some small inkling. If you don't choose your moments, they are often chosen for you. More's the pity.

"Who are you, sir?" asked the judge.

"My name is Vincent Ainge, I'm a mitigation investigator. Mr. Merck is my client."

Abby's hands went to her mouth and covered it. What came out of Arnie Stimick was a lot like a shriek. A wound had been inflicted, salt poured inside it. "What! You son of a bitch!" I don't remember what else he called Vincent, because the other Friends of Eileen were gasping and sputtering and the room itself seemed to shudder.

"Order!" demanded the judge. "I will clear this courtroom. Order, and *now*. Do you have something pertinent to this?" he asked Vincent.

"I believe Mr. Merck is overreacting to the sessions I had with him. He may have misinterpreted some of my remarks to him. His plea is impulsive and irrational and self-destructive, like the rest of his life, Your Honor. What's more, it is contrary to the plans of his legal defense."

"I know what I'm doing," said Randy. "This is gonna be a better world without the likes of Randy Merck in it. *That's* my contribution."

Abby stood up and reached back for her purse. She quickly left the courtroom. Reluctantly, Arnie followed her. Vincent turned and watched her leave, taking any hope of a future that included him.

"Your Honor," said Wendy, finding her voice at last, "may we have a recess so that I can confer with my client and my investigators?"

Granted, and after elbowing our way through the press and spectators, and the Friends of Eileen hissing "Traitor!" at Vincent again and again, we made it to a conference room.

28

"Randy, what the hell are you doing?" This from Vincent.

Wendy held her head in her hands, so undone.

"I'm making a contribution. I thought you'd be happy, I'm accepting responsibility."

"You told him to accept responsibility?" asked Wendy, incredulous.

"After a fashion."

"Who told you to tell him that? In any fashion."

"I didn't tell him to commit suicide."

"It's time to call it a day," said Randy.

"Wendy, he may have killed others, many others."

"I don't want to hear about it!"

"He may be the Aurora Slasher."

"Shut the fuck up! Shut the fuck up! Don't say another fucking word!" Her voice was so shrill.

Randy chuckled.

"Wendy," I said, "calm down. Hear what he has to say."

"We're here with a serial killer," he said. "Randy?" Randy did not deny it. "Randy, are you or are you not the Aurora Slasher?"

"Maybe I am . . . and maybe I'm not. Anyway, it's over."

"Oh, it's over all right," said Wendy. "It's definitely over. I will not be ridiculed this way in open court. Get yourself another lawyer, asshole."

"Don't need one now," said Randy.

"And you," she said, jabbing her finger at Vincent. "You're finished. Find yourself another line of work, your career is over. There won't be a defense lawyer in the Northwest willing to trust you."

"We'll see. Right now we have a bigger problem to deal with."

"Not *we,* asshole, not we."

It was a moment, for her, during which everyone else had become an asshole.

"Look," said Randy, trying to make peace, "I'm okay with this. If you want to know the truth, I feel pretty good."

"Oh, you feel pretty good," said Wendy, dripping with sarcasm.

"I do. I feel, like, totally all right with this."

"Well, that's just dandy, Randy. But this

whole process isn't about your cleansing your fucking soul."

Randy looked at her blankly.

"It's about saving your life, Randy," Vincent told him.

"What's it to you, whether I live or not?"

"It's everything," said Vincent.

Randy squinted. He didn't get it. How could saving his worthless life be everything to anybody?

29

I'll admit I don't really understand our justice system. I've never met anyone who does, not really. The process of the system has long overtaken the purpose of it. Justice is not the goal. I know everyone says that, but then what is the goal? The goal is that the process be followed, and if justice happens, cool; if it's injustice that occurs, well, that's a pity, but at least the proper steps were followed.

If a defendant pleads guilty when his lawyer wants him to plead not guilty, then there has been a foul-up in the process and that cannot be tolerated. Judge Anderson was pissed.

After we regrouped and returned from the recess, Wendy asked to be taken off the case, which in her opinion had been sabotaged by her own MI, her investigator, and her client. Judge Anderson did a slow burn. He spoke directly to Randy.

"Mr. Merck, I will not accept your guilty plea. In my opinion, you do not know what you are doing. You have a fine attorney representing you. I suggest you listen to her. We will resume in three days' time, after which I expect a proper plea and an end to these shenanigans."

I got to talk to Vincent for a few minutes as he crossed the bridge to go back and meet with Randy and Wendy, but all he could talk about was Abby and what she must be thinking. I didn't waste my breath telling him I told you so.

I knew I didn't want to spend any more time with Randy, and I wasn't all that thrilled to pass an afternoon with Wendy, or with Vincent, for that matter. I went back to my office. I thought maybe I'd hit the sofa, hope the hot flash currently peeling me from within would take a break.

I pulled up my collar and walked through the rain.

Out of the elevator, on my floor, I shook the rain off my hair and unbuttoned my raincoat.

A bench positioned against the rail, under the skylight, was common ground. Most of the offices were one-room affairs, like mine, and anyone waiting in line, or just waiting, was free to sit on the bench. So the man sitting there could have been waiting for anyone, but I knew he was waiting for me.

"Mr. Voss, I presume," I said.

He was as Randy had described him, except he was closer to sixty than fifty. He wore a blue raincoat, a black beret, and shades, even though the sun hadn't been out in weeks.

"And you must be Quinn."

"How do you know me?"

He shrugged. No big deal. I guess not, since I'd been asking about him all over Bremerton.

"I need to tell you a couple of things."

His voice had a whiskey rasp and an evil quaver. I was not keen on being alone with this creep, though in a fair fight you'd be wise to put your money on me. Still, I couldn't talk to him out in the atrium, so I asked him into my office.

"So tell me," I said.

"Can I sit down?"

"Sure."

He did; I didn't. I stood behind my desk. I unlocked my desk drawer and opened it so that my LadySmith would be close at hand. To that point I had never shot a man, but I wouldn't have minded if Mr. Voss turned out to be the first.

He sat down, stretched out his legs, and

crossed them at the feet. He wrapped his arms at his chest.

"I heard Randy pled guilty."

"That was fast."

"Was on the radio."

"And you're here why?"

"He didn't do it."

"Who did, you?"

"Neither one of us. We found a car. We hopped in. Wrong car, I guess."

I told him to start at the beginning and he told essentially the same story that Randy had, in the beginning, before he decided that maybe he did commit the murder. They had run into each other, had a beer at one of Seattle's more gruesome watering holes, prowled the streets, and wound up finding an open and ready car in Capitol Hill. They took the car and stayed high until paranoia set in, at which time all roads led to Canada. But by the time Mr. Voss got back to the car, Randy was busted. No sense both of them going down. Mr. Voss took it on the arfy-darfy.

"While your protégé and rent boy got hit with a murder rap," I said.

"Quite a shock. Randy is a vicious little package, and I'm not saying it wouldn't have happened eventually, but to date Randy has killed no one."

"Why didn't you come forward?"

"Well, we did steal a car, technically."

"Car theft in King County is like somewhere below poker on the crime scale. You have to steal six of them before you do any time."

"Exactly. I figured it was the most they could stick Randy with, and since he had blown off the halfway house and broken parole he was going back to Walla Walla anyway, but not for long, and he never minded it much before, so . . . but I can't let the boy do this. He's flipped. He wants to commit suicide by state. Plus, I'm sure he likes the attention, and my guess is he's met someone that he's trying to please. Maybe you."

Vincent.

"Why didn't you go to the police. Why me?"

"You were looking for me. The police weren't."

Now I did sit down. What was I going to do with this?

Almost from the beginning my gut instinct had told me Randy wasn't the killer, but the torture of his childhood all but blinded me to my own instinct. He did have a long record of assaults, after all, and there was the confession and the guilty plea, and the demand for the death penalty, which should have tipped me off, but like everyone else I was too far into accepting what seemed obvious, a mistake I hope not to make in the future.

With Randy off the list, there were not, in my mind, a lot of other possibilities. It could have been some other random killer, but those creeps almost always use a weapon, another element I'd put out of my mind once Randy confessed. I'd once looked hard at Guy, the boyfriend, but he didn't have the strength to crush a pineapple. Bernard? Forget about it. Eileen was killed by a big man obsessed with her youth and beauty, someone powerful enough and maybe unhinged enough to take her into his arms and squeeze the life out of her. I knew two who could fill that profile: Arnie Stimick and Vincent Ainge. It hurt my heart to have to consider it.

"What now?" asked the pervert.

"Do you have a place to stay tonight?"

"The Shangri-la, out on Aurora."

No stranger juxtaposition of names exists. I knew the place. One step down from the missions but a step up from the streets.

I gave him twenty bucks.

"Sit tight. Stay there until I call you. If I don't call you by this time tomorrow, you contact this person."

I gave him Wendy's card.

I owed Vincent that much.

30

After sending Mr. Voss back to the Shangri-la, I sat alone for an hour thinking of the weeks, now months, wasted on Randy Merck, nutter, while the actual killer was hiding in plain sight, and maybe even from himself.

I left the building by the front door and crossed to the left to see what my Indians were up to.

There were only two of them tonight, and one of them asked me for a cigarette.

"Don't smoke. Where's your friend?"

"Takin' a piss."

I turned and looked at the parking lot, and sure enough here comes the skinny one zipping up his fly.

Passing him, I went up James to the Korean store and bought a carton of Salems. I brought them back to the bench under the pergola and tossed the carton onto the lap of the middle one. They tore into it.

"You always piss in the parking lot?" I asked them.

"Is that wrong?"

"Just curious."

They all nodded. That was their bathroom of choice.

"You're here all night, every night. Ain't?"

They agreed that was mostly true.

"One of you pisses, the other two guard the turf?"

It only seemed natural, they said, and of course they were wondering why I cared.

"And during the night you're over there, what, two three times?"

"Four, five times, sometimes."

"Gentlemen, I'm going to ask you to do something for me. It might be hard."

They wanted to know what.

"Remember."

31

In the middle of the night I stood at my window. They were my Indians now and their chanting was not an annoyance. This time they settled for less and were happier with what they knew than with what they could never recapture. They all smoked the cigarettes I had given them and the fat one beat a cardboard box and the skinny one chanted.

I'd spent most of the night poring over computerized records, finally finding the right name in the right slot, but it was a name that I didn't recognize until I realized that, like most things in life that don't make sense, you have to read it right to know it. Gerry McNamara. Didn't know him from Adam. But a quick Google and I knew who killed Eileen Jones, and I thought I knew why.

The police, of course, were always going to like Randy Merck, and he did confess, which is powerful evidence to most jurors. Anyone who's actually worked in crime knows that a confession doesn't count for beans. His pleading guilty would certainly seem to seal the deal, but even that cannot be relied upon in the face of stronger opposing evidence.

The evidence I had, relying in part on the memory of three drunken Indians and my gut instincts, was not what you could call strong. Another piece or two, though, and I was home. In the morning, I decided, I would call Sergeant Beckman and tell him what I'd uncovered.

Morning came a little late that day for me. For the first time in weeks, when I finally did hit the pillow, I was out. I slept until eleven. I called Sergeant Beckman and left a long message telling him what I knew. I scrambled into my clothes, did what I could with my hair, slapped on a little lipstick, and was out the door.

I went to Vincent's office first, but he wasn't there. It occurred to me that it was Friday, his day with his father. I called his cell phone. No answer. It was seldom I could get an answer on his cell because he was always forgetting it somewhere.

I went up to Arnie Stimick's office, but he wasn't there. One of the girls told me he'd gone to the island to look after Abby, after the trauma of yesterday's court scene. I went down to Bernard's office, but he wasn't there, either.

Finally I went to my own office, looked up the number of the Beeliner Diner, and called there, hoping to catch Vincent and his father at lunch. The waitress hadn't seen them. I called the rest home and was told that Vincent had picked up his dad as usual.

I leaned back in my chair and wondered where they were. God, no. He wouldn't. Sure, he would. He'd gone to the island. Like Arnie, he would want to look after Abby, to explain himself to her, beg her forgiveness. I looked through my book and called Abby's number. The phone rang a dozen times. She had no answering machine or service. I ran back to the apartment house and took the elevator to parking. I checked my watch. I had ten minutes to catch the ferry.

32

I remembered the way to her house. As I drove there, the rain stopped and I was able to drive without wipers. I found the dead-end road and her driveway. From the top of the driveway I could see two cars parked side by side: Vincent's Trooper and Stimick's Range Rover. Abby's car, I figured, must be in the garage. I had an urge to park at the end of the dead-end road and walk back, maybe circle the house and come in from the water side. You should follow your instincts. But everything looked peaceful and there was no reason why it shouldn't be, once Abby and Arnie got over a justified sense of betrayal.

I pulled into the gravel driveway and parked behind Arnie. I threw my purse over my shoulder, undid the flap, and rested my hand inside it, around my LadySmith. I rang the bell. In a moment Abby answered. She didn't look glad to see me.

"Sorry to come unannounced," I said. "I see you have company."

"You might as well come on in."

I took off my shoes in the entry, a common practice in wet climates. I saw Vincent's shoes already there. I bent over to untie my Rockports, taking my hand out of my purse, and that was a mistake. A beat too slow, I wondered where Arnie's shoes were.

Still on his feet. He was beyond such niceties. His automatic pressed against the base of my skull. He took my purse.

"Get up."

I stood erect, my hands above my head.

"Turn around."

He was wearing a down vest. Out of one of the zippered pockets the head of a remote phone emerged. On the wood floor behind him were the pieces of another phone. He took the LadySmith from my purse and put that into another pocket. He motioned me to walk toward him as he backed up, slid open the glass door, and threw my cell phone toward the bay. If he made it, I didn't hear the splash.

On the sofa, next to the loom, Vincent sat with his hands in front of him, a plastic tie binding his hands together. It looked like his nose was broken.

"Quinn, Quinn, Quinn," he said. His voice

314

sounded different. The nose.

I wanted to tell him not to Quinn me, but my throat was dry.

"Another strip, please," Arnie said to Abby. "Make it two."

She reached into the mudroom and came out with two of the plastic ties she used in her gardening.

"Do her."

Abby tightened the strip around my wrists. It would have made such sense, I thought, to have come around the house, gun in hand, and control this situation. Now here I was, SOL.

"Sit down."

I sat next to Vincent.

Arnie put his automatic into his waistband and fastened a strip around Abby's wrists. Lady? I thought. Lady? Grab the friggin' gun. Do something. But all she did was dutifully extend her arms.

Abby sat next to me. We sat like the three monkeys. Abby heard no evil, Vincent saw no evil, and I, at the moment, was speaking no evil. Arnie leveled his gun at our heads. I had to believe that somehow this madness would turn around and find traction. Stimick was not an extraordinary man. I figured he'd come over to the island to comfort Abby and ingratiate himself, but when he ran into Vincent he lost it and cold-cocked him, probably after putting it together that the traitor and Abby were intimate. Arnie was blustery. He was self-righteous. He made a lot of noise, displaced a lot of air, made a big wake. But he had no reason to shoot anybody in the face, especially any of us. Or all of us. That's what I was thinking. Hoping.

He sat down in the rocking chair, the coffee table between us. Despite his controlled exterior, I could see that he was roiling within and confused about what to do, having created this situation. It was, after all, the kind of tableau that gave hard-ons to every SWAT team in the land: man with a gun, three hostages.

Now he cradled the gun against his other arm and rocked nervously.

Vincent said, "Look, Stimick, he's not going to get away with this, believe me. All I want is that his sentence be life without parole."

Stimick seemed not to be listening.

"Is the process more important than justice?" Vincent posed, like an oily politician. "I guess it is. I guess it has to be, because without a fair and established process, there won't be any justice. You're still working through your grief, Stimick.

Oh, God, who can't see it? Who can't recognize it? Grief." Vincent looked like he was thinking a little bit about grief, remembering it, bringing it back. "Grief is like the brother you haven't seen since Mom died. He shows up at your apartment in the middle of the night and misses the toilet when he pees. He borrows money and smokes your cigars. He gets the password to your PowerBook and reads your e-mail."

"You're so fucking cute."

He was too fucking cute, by half. But mitigating was his business and his path. He needed to say the right word, the right three little words, the right sentence to save our lives. Unless Stimick was insane, which was certainly a possibility, our lives should not have been in danger. Not if all of this was about Randy's pleading guilty and Vincent's not letting him. Again, I was hoping that's what it was about.

"You've caused more grief than you've ever suffered, you silly son of a bitch and your brother," said Stimick.

"I wish I could deny it. It's a moot point, anyway. And I don't have a brother, by the way. But here's the thing. Here is the thing, and it's very important. You want to hear the thing?" Stimick didn't say, so Vincent told him the thing anyway: "I haven't caused your grief, and neither has Abby here."

Da frick. What about me?

I don't pray but I found myself saying, Let this be about Stimick's grief and sorrow and shame. Felt like a prayer.

"You just love to talk, don't you?" Stimick said.

"Not really." I knew that to be true. "Really, I don't much care for talk. I love the silences between talk, and I love silences all by themselves. Only, at times like this, Stimick . . . you've got to talk. I don't want you to destroy yourself. What a waste that would be."

"Destroy myself? By blowing you away? I would do about three years in prison, maybe less."

He was right. With a good case for diminished capacity, temporary insanity, and a clever lawyer to argue it, a man like Stimick might not even have to go to prison. His every behavior, from the start of it all, had been obsessive, and one of the strongest obsessions of them all, that of a middle-aged man for a pretty teenage girl. Yes, the female jurors might want to hang him, just for that, and it might hurt to have fathers on the panel, but all you need is that one aging man who has also confused youth with

beauty, beauty with contentment, contentment with joy. A man like my ex-husband.

33

Day turned to murky twilight, and Stimick allowed Vincent to talk, almost aimlessly, digging for the right words in the perfect sequence. They were, as always, elusive. Much of the time he spent mitigating all over again for Randy, for the value of all human life, indirectly including his own. He talked of meeting Eileen and the impression she made upon him, how he felt he had known her all his life, maybe even before that, in a previous life. He talked of his father, of their weekly lunch dates, of watching him disappear in bits and drabs. He told Stimick of his own fears of likewise losing it. He told him of all the houses and apartments he had lived in, all over the city, of his failed marriage to a flaky woman who had resumed, just a few years after marrying Vincent, the love affair she'd had with a much older man. He talked about how difficult it was to have any human relationships, given the work he does. How he hoped and dreamed it might be different with Abby, but how he understood and perhaps always knew that it wouldn't be. It was a long narrative and if it did nothing else at least it calmed Stimick, who once or twice looked at me and I looked away.

The wind changed directions and was blowing in from the north, which Abby told us was uncommon. The north wind always brings the worst storms. Salt spray was pelting hard against the seawall. On the upland side of Abby's house, the tall cedars swayed in widening arcs. The wind roared through the branches like a swollen river in the sky.

Stimick turned on the small portable TV on the kitchen counter, but there was no reception.

"What's the matter with this thing? I can't get a clear picture."

"The cable is out, because of the wind," Abby told him.

He turned off the TV and sat again on the rocker in the living room, facing us. The automatic lay flat on his open hand. He looked at it vacantly. Then he bolted upright at what sounded like a rifle shot from outside. "What the hell . . . ?"

"It's just a tree branch cracking," Abby told him. "We have to hope a tree doesn't fall down on us."

"Who cares?" he said, reaching up and turning on a floor lamp.

"I should fill up the two bathtubs."

"You want to take a *bath*? Now?"

"No, we have to store some water. If the power goes off, the water stops. I'm on a well, with an electric pump. We won't be able to flush the toilets."

"You ought to have a generator," Vincent suggested.

"I don't like having gasoline around."

"Oh. Yes, that could be dangerous. Can I do anything to help?"

"You could fill up the tub in the master bath. I'll do the guest bath."

"No you won't," said Stimick.

"We should also fill the kettle and a couple of the big pots, and put them on the stove, in case we want hot water."

"Your stove won't work, either, will it?" I asked.

"The stove will work fine. It's propane."

"Really?" said Vincent. "Then you ought to get a propane generator, hook it right up to your propane tank."

"I *hate* this kind of talk!" Stimick moaned, casting his eyes to the ceiling.

"It's called living," I said, a superior edge to my voice.

"You'll start in about the" — his head swiveled, looking for an example — "about the goddamn *flowers* next."

"I was going to ask about that," I said. "I havn't seen narcissus done that way before, inside like you have them." I was messing with him.

"Oh, sure, you just rest the bulbs on pebbles and keep them wet," Abby said.

"But don't the stalks fall over?"

"Well, yes, eventually. You can tie them, but —"

"Stop it! You're driving me crazy!"

"Life is not about the big things, Arnie," I said. "It's about narcissus and propane and the power going out, and having enough water if it does."

"Just shut up about it! Nobody's filling anything. We won't be here that long."

"Oh, yeah," I said. "Where're we going?"

"I think you know."

I did. All that I was hoping this was about? It wasn't, and I knew why.

"I'll tell you what I do," said Vincent, quickly, as though his narrative had only been interrupted, "for my living and for my life. It's nothing clever. I look for one true sentence that a jury can hear that might save a person's life."

Stimick continued to look at me, let's say

fatally. Vincent must have sensed it. That's why he took an urgent refuge in his monologue.

"I try this one, I try that one, and then if I'm lucky I stumble across the right one. I never know what it might be, but there is always a simple statement of truth that can change the mind of even the most resolute."

Now Stimick turned back to him. Huh?

"No flowery phrase from a lawyer's grab bag will work, just a simple declarative statement that connects the convicted with those who would decide his fate."

"Give me an example," Stimick said flatly.

"Okay. Once I convinced a reluctant lawyer to put a convicted killer's eight-year-old son on the stand for just one question and one answer. The question was asked and the answer came in three little words, and I knew I had saved the man's life."

"What was it? The question?"

"The lawyer pointed at the defendant and asked the boy, 'Do you know this man?' "

"And what was the answer?"

"The boy looked at the convicted killer and said, 'That's my daddy.' "

"I don't get it."

"That was the one right sentence. 'That's my daddy.' It made the jury realize that although they wanted to retaliate against

324

the killer, they did not want to retaliate against an innocent eight-year-old boy."

"But you don't have a little boy, do you?"

"I did. I had a little boy. Now it's just me and my father, and sometimes in the morning when I wake up I hope that he died peacefully in his sleep."

"That's a shit thing to say about your own father."

"I know it is, but it's true, and I'm trying to be honest here. You can be honest, too. You loved Eileen, didn't you, Arnie?"

"Isn't that clear?"

"She filled a void in your life."

"Don't take off on my life, asshole. My life was good. Okay, by some standards, maybe it hasn't amounted to much. My work is pretty much a scam . . . don't have a wife or child . . . but those girls . . . we called them 'Arnie's Angels' . . . and Eileen especially, they made my life worth living. Eileen made life worth living. Yes, I loved her."

"Did you? Or were you obsessed with her?"

"Obsessed?"

"Looks like obsession to me."

"We had a very special relationship."

"Because . . . I was obsessed with her," said Vincent.

"What?" Abby couldn't believe what she'd heard.

And it rattled Stimick. It didn't do much for me, either.

"She filled a void in my life, too. I was afraid to breathe. There was just something about her, something fresh and new, and yet something wise and old, something sweet and simple, yet daring and complicated," Vincent said.

"What are you telling me?" asked Stimick.

"That I understand, a little, about obsession. I accept it. I make no judgments. But I understand about boundaries, too. Didn't you? I could be obsessed with her in my world . . . but not in hers."

"Did you ever touch my daughter?" Abby asked him.

"No. I could look, but I could not touch. That's the boundary."

"Can you say the same, Arnie?" I said.

His right arm lay on the arm of the rocking chair, the gun in his hand. He moved his left hand over to support it at the wrist.

"Abby . . . ," he said, "I am ashamed to my marrow. I am so, so sorry and mortified. None of this should ever have happened."

"How about cutting these strips, Arnie?" said Vincent. "Let's call it a day, get home before the storm hits, and we can mull this over another day."

"Can't do that."

"Sure you can. Why not?"

"Quinn knows."

"Quinn? Why can't he?"

"Beats me," I said. "Sounds like a good idea, before things get out of hand."

"Things are already way out of hand," said Stimick. "Sergeant Beckman called me. On my way over here. Everything changed then."

"He called you?" Like I had to ask. How else could this have happened?

"I told you before, I'm friends with the cops. They all know me."

If I live to get out of this, I thought, they're going to know me, too. Even if Beckman thought I was up the wrong tree, he had no right to tip off my suspect.

"What is going on?" Abby asked, reasonably.

"I'd like to know, too," said Vincent.

It started to rain now, and the wind kept building.

"Go ahead, Quinn. Tell them."

I shifted over on one haunch and looked down the sofa at Vincent.

"Mr. Voss showed up at my office."

"He lives?"

"Yeah, he's real. If not otherworldly."

"Who's Mr. Voss?" asked Abby.

"It's a long story, but he's Randy's alibi. Randy Merck didn't kill your daughter. His confession was false. His guilty plea was bogus, and he's one sick individual, though maybe not as sick as some, who hide it so much better."

I bore a hole into Arnie with my eyes.

"Then who did kill her?" she asked.

"Arnie did. Why, we may never know, but it starts with the obsession they were talking about."

No denial from Stimick. He couldn't even look at us. He really was ashamed, but not so ashamed that he would try to make amends.

"I mean, how do you suspect the most bereaved, the founder of the Friends of Eileen, a man who hired a PI first to find her, then to find her killer? That bit was based on his belief that I didn't know my ass from my elbow. He thought I was dumb. I was a woman, so I was halfway there anyway. And he wanted me on the job so that he could know what the police knew. Sad to say, that worked."

Arnie wasn't talking. "Go on," Vincent said.

"Under the pergola, in Pioneer Square, three street people have taken up residence.

Indians, they are, the drunk kind, who try to remember songs from their heritage. When they're not doing that, when they're not pissing in the parking lot across the street, they amuse themselves by calling out the makes and models of passing cars. They have their favorites. One of them is queer for Range Rovers. Especially likes yours, Arnie, and whenever he goes over to the lot to take a piss, he pauses to admire your ride. Even thought about stealing it one night, because usually it's gone by six, but this night it was there till eleven, till midnight, till two in the morning. He gave some serious thought to stealing it, but he didn't, because guess what? He's an honest man. He only *thinks* about his bad impulses, like Vincent here. You? You're different that way.

"That night the car was left until two, before you came back to claim it. That was the night Eileen disappeared. Now, my Indians might not be the best of witnesses. They're hopeless drunks, after all, but of this they were sure. Still, I wouldn't want to hang a man based on their testimony, so I went and checked out the taxi company that brought the big man back to his beautiful Range Rover. Save their souls, they couldn't remember which cab company it was. Hell, there aren't that many in Seattle, so I took them one at a time. It wasn't that hard, they're all computerized now, and they were fine with me sitting in an office and running down a fare from where the car was left on Capitol Hill to the parking lot in Pioneer Square, sometime between one and two in the morning. Lo and behold, I found one.

"Somebody by the name of Gerry Mc-Namara. Now, I don't know this individual, but I think I know who's using his name. When a person has to use an alias on impulse, he either comes up with something that sounds a lot like his real name or he blurts out a name that's on his mind for some reason. I used the cab company's computer to Google 'Gerry McNamara.' There's more than one, but one dominates. That's the basketball star from Syracuse University, Stimick's alma mater. This Mc-Namara kid is who Stimick always wanted to be."

I turned to him and said, "I ran down the cabdriver who picked you up that night. Described you to a T."

I enjoyed a moment of stunned silence.

"Motive? Middle-aged man's obsession with a young girl, a subject I know something about. Yeah, you took all the girls out to dinner 'cause you were such a good boss, but that was the only way you could make believe you were out on a date with Eileen, the object of your fantasies.

"That night, you left work early, you waited for her at her car. Maybe you told her you couldn't start your car. Of course she'd give you a ride. No way of knowing what went on during that ride. Maybe you confessed your love and she recoiled and you saw in her eyes just what you were. Or maybe she told you she loved someone else, maybe she told you that she was in love with two people simultaneously and that was an affront your tight ass couldn't handle. Whatever. Whatever she said, you took her into your arms and you crushed her. You put your arm around her neck and you strangled her. You dumped her out of the car and took the car to Capitol Hill, where you parked it and left the keys inside, where Randy and Mr. Voss found it. Then you called for a cab, went back and got your own car."

Arnie had nothing to say.

"Altogether, not a bad case. So I did the right thing, which turned out to be the wrong thing. I called the police, who were way too wed to Randy as the killer. I mean, he confessed, pled guilty, and asked for the gallows. What more could you ask? Enough for them. And everybody at the station knows Arnie, he's a good guy. Well, you're not a good guy, Arnie. You're a sick killer."

"I can mitigate the hell out of this, Arnie," said Vincent. "It's a slam dunk. You won't have to hang."

"I'd almost rather, but I can't, and I can't spend my life in prison. I can't. I have to do this. I'm sorry. What more can I say?"

Abby was weeping, gone really, no longer among us. Nothing worse could happen to her. I wasn't afraid of death, but I've always had a healthy fear of dying and planned to go down fighting. Vincent I couldn't speak for, and he seemed to have run out of words himself.

"Think about it, Arnie," I said. "You kill one of us, you got to kill all of us. Whole thing might look a tad, like, suspicious?"

"You made it possible, just by showing up," he said to me.

He took my LadySmith out of his vest pocket and put his automatic in its place, zippered up the pocket.

I looked at my gun in his hand and figured it out.

He checked the chambers. Some people like to leave the first one empty. I wasn't one of them.

"You came in here," he said, "like a wild

person, shot this weirdo and Abby dead, wounded me. But I was able to get off a shot and kill you."

"Why would I do that? Go wild?" I asked.

"Why does anybody do anything? I'm guessing somewhere in your past you freaked out once or twice."

Indeed.

He leveled the gun at Vincent's face.

Vincent shut his eyes and then opened them again, wide. "I'd like to call my father, if you don't mind."

"Why?"

"To say good-bye."

Who would have guessed that among the infinite arrangements of three little words, those three would work?

Stimick took the phone out of his vest and handed it to Vincent.

"Go ahead."

"Please, Arnie, don't. Don't do this," murmured Abby.

"Too late now, Abby. I'll make it quick."

Vincent punched out the numbers. I kept an eye on Abby. She looked like a woman on the shore, watching someone caught in the undertow. Vincent kept his ear to the phone, waiting. It rang again and again.

"What's taking so long?"

"Probably nobody at the nurses' station

right now. They always answer eventually."

The front door swung open and, ta-da! Vincent's disoriented father was standing there holding his ringing cell phone. "How do you turn this damn thing off?" he asked, holding it at arm's length.

Stimick's jaw dropped.

Vincent threw the phone at Arnie, catching the side of his head, drawing blood. I jumped over the coffee table and made a grab for the gun. I covered it with my two hands, my wrists bound, and twisted it in his hand. Vincent was just an instant behind me, and both of us were on the big man, trying to wrestle him down. He flailed this way and that, trying to shake us off, but we hung on. Vincent tried to loop his hands over his head to garrote him. I tried to ram my knee into his soft spot but kept hitting his thigh instead. He dragged us toward Clinton in the entryway. Vincent gave up on the garrote and jammed his forearm into Stimick's throat. We all fell to the floor. I had his gun hand in both of mine, and I hit it against the hardwood floor, again and again, trying to knock the gun loose. Six legs kicked and flailed, struggling for leverage.

Clinton moved out of the way and looked on, bewildered, the ringing phone still in his hand. It stopped ringing when Abby retrieved the remote and dialed 911. Clinton laid the cell phone on the dining table and stood watching us, as though we were a show on TV.

Stimick braced his back against the entry closet door and tried to get to his feet, but I wrapped a leg behind him and pulled, turned, and pushed until we went down again, but I landed below Stimick and Vincent landed on top of him. The weight of them both knocked the wind out of me and dislocated my shoulder. The gun went loose and clattered across the hardwood to Clinton's feet. I looked at it in desperation, unable to move, unable to breathe.

Abby was on the phone describing in a ragged hoarse voice all that she was seeing, yelling into the phone for someone to come. "There's an intruder with a gun!"

Only now the gun was in the hands of old man Ainge, an Alzheimer's patient. He examined it curiously. Was he trying to figure out just what it was? A radio? An electric razor? Vincent still struggled with Stimick. I was fighting for air. I slid on my back toward Clinton and the gun.

Stimick was returning to full strength. His big hands tightened around Vincent's throat, cutting off his air. Vincent tried to break the hold with his bound hands, but he was falling into unconsciousness. With what little breath I had, I yelled to Clinton, "Shoot him! Shoot him! Shoot him!" Clinton must have heard me, because he pointed the gun.

Vincent gasped, "No!"

Now, I have to make this clear: Vincent wasn't crying, No, don't shoot me. He was saying, No, don't shoot *him.* Don't shoot anybody. Which says all anyone has to know about compassion.

But the old man found the trigger and fired. The bullet splintered the wood next to Stimick's head. It rattled him enough for Vincent to twist out of his grip and jab him with his elbow, right in the breadbasket. Vincent took a breath and hit him again. He was drilling him with quick two-handed elbow punches to the stomach.

For a brief and glorious moment, I thought he was in control, but Clinton leveled the gun again, and again Vincent cried, "No!" The old man fired and this one hit Vincent. The blow of the shot lifted him away from Stimick and landed him against the low windowsill. He sat there in disbelief, looking down at the hole in his chest.

Stimick fell to his knees. Still on my back, I kicked up and caught him on the chin, which sent his head banging against the wall. I struggled to my feet and took the gun away from the old man. Now I was definitely in charge. I could have held Stimick under gunpoint until the cops showed up. And of course I did, but in the meantime I fired off a round smack into his butt. I'm a piss-poor shot but you didn't have to be a sharpshooter to hit that target. I wanted him to limp on his way up the hangman's scaffold.

Stimick's leg snapped out involuntarily. He rolled over and wailed like a lost toddler, unmanned by the excruciating pain.

Honestly, I wanted to laugh, but I didn't have the air for it, and a good man lay dying. I took Stimick's automatic out of his vest pocket, popped the magazine, and cleared the chamber. I handed it to the old man.

Stimick was still wailing. Clinton studied the gun again. Was it a fedora? A love seat? A rascally puppy? He looked at the men on the floor, one of them lying quiet and vaguely familiar to him, the other a complete stranger sending up a fuss.

And there's me, with Vincent in my arms.

34

An hour after it all happened, Clinton had no recollection of the shooting. An island cop took him onto the ferry and a Seattle cop picked him up and took him back to the rest home. He introduced the officer to Howard the Magnificent as his son. Howard quizzed him on his name and his uniform, but the old boy ducked the questions. Vincent didn't show up the next Friday as he usually did, and Clinton didn't seem to miss him.

Since by now I knew all the moves, and to honor Vincent's memory, I mitigated for Stimick. There are always two ways to look at things, I testified, at least two. Arnold Stimick, in all that he had done after his crime of passion, was either the world's worst hypocrite or he was trying already to atone for what he had done. I put together a mitigation folder for him that was a work of art. Vincent would have been proud.

I could have taken over Vincent's practice, I guess, but deep down I know there are always going to be some killers whose ticket ought to be punched. There are certain individuals who ought to get on to the next life and start all over again, preferably as Norwegian roof rats. So I said good-bye to Vincent and all mitigating circumstances and went back to snooping and drooping.

Stimick? He's got a Walla Walla suite for life, a room with no view.

I should care.

AFTERWORD

Readers familiar with Seattle will notice my failure to acknowledge certain changes in the physical and social landscape of that city. The writing of this book took so long that some of the terrain changed before its completion. Out of a perverse commemorative sense, I am loath to accept that nothing lasts forever, and so in my Seattle some things never change. I may have tweaked the architecture as well. On balance, readers should have no argument with the climate.

ABOUT THE AUTHOR

Anne Argula was born and raised in Shenandoah, Pennsylvania, an anthracite coal-mining town. She currently lives in Seattle. This is her second novel in the Quinn series.